PAWN QUEST

PAWN QUEST

BOOK ONE

KATE HARRINGTON

PART ONE

DODGE

He was Spider. He wielded the remaining threads of his grandfather's empire.

At his command, the opaque wall of his penthouse apartment became transparent to reveal a gradually brightening sky and the rooftops of neighboring arcologies, each arcology a stepped pyramid, each step obscured by trees. They should have retained their original stark Meso-American flavor, but no, the residents demanded their gardens.

Spider sipped his java (though Java the island had not grown coffee in well over a century). Gourmands claimed coffee and chocolate were nothing like they'd been in the past. No matter. He knew what he liked. His food fabricator produced the perfect hot drink every time.

With a thought, he activated his tooth phone. "Tech."

1

"Here." The answer came, slow, sluggish. Caught Tech sleeping, had he? So what? He owned Tech, who was his lifeline to the National Online Data Exchange. He owned the NODE, though the country might disagree!

"What news?" Spider asked.

A stifled yawn. "Your data check out. All but number eight. That one just declared emancipation and moved to Workless. Age . . . fifteen."

Spider reviewed his list. "Have a watch set on him, via your usual channels."

When Tech remained silent, Spider began to pace. A slosh of java hit the creamy carpet, to be sensed and obliterated by his house system. "Well?"

"He has to check into the employment office twice a week." Tech sounded reluctant. "And he's far from being of age. No need for haste."

"I said a *watch*. I want to know who he sees, what he does, where he goes. He could be useful."

"Will do."

Tech was too squeamish. A pity those kids had been allowed to live. But this particular disposable kid had certain talents and might prove useful.

Ran

Ran Kenelm stomped out of the Dodge City Employment Office. "Nothing today, kid." Always the same. So what if he was only fifteen? He could fix any machine—intelligent or mechanical.

He'd left his foster home on impulse, fed up with being bossed around. After all, everyone was guaranteed food and shelter.

Big mistake.

Dodge City did indeed provide shelter and two meals a day—but not forever.

He clenched his fists. He had dug this hole himself, his very own black hole of stupidity. Helping out at Sam's Antiques, the one bright spot of his days, didn't solve his problem. He had to get a real job. Two more months without finding a job and he'd end up on the road crew demolishing old Highway 70.

"You don't look ahead," his foster father always said. Yeah, but he had. Maybe he'd looked too far ahead. Maybe he didn't know anything. Nothing of use, that was sure. Neither his real name, nor his genetics, nor why . . .

He headed back down Gunsmoke Street, where corner news boxes blared out headlines, enticing passersby to pay for details, humming with the faint vibration that said all was well. But the You Are Here map guide was dark. Ran paused, slid his hand along the underside of the unit. Nope, nothing he could fix. The power pack had been ripped out. Probably stolen by noids—the only people not chipped, untraceable—though they didn't usually steal this close to City Center.

A pedal-powered sausage cart squeaked past. It needed oil. His mouth watering, Ran angled across Boot Hill Plaza, drawing side-glances and some double takes at his gray coverall because school kids wore blue. A group of primary school children followed their teacher into the museum that enclosed ancient storefronts inside climate-controlled walls. Ran had done the same at that age, an actual non-virtual experience. Shops lined two other sides of the plaza and on the fourth side was the library.

A bearded man in old-fashioned cowboy vest talked from the soapbox, though people passing by paid him no attention. "Half of Earth closed off to human settlement—"

Yeah, yeah. Kids accepted that reality, but adults still protested the decades-old World Court order to vacate half of every continent, allowing plants and animals free access to spread and evolve in the new norm.

--"so now they fill more and more arcologies with their families"—

Well, *duh!* Rising oceans, coastal storms, who could blame people for moving—within human boundaries, of course. Ran's respect for machines extended to arcologies, those self-sufficient communities consisting of quarter-mile-square, truncated pyramids. Their inhabitants never had to touch the ground, free to fly away, or walk connecting bridges to other arcologies.

"Ship 'em off-planet instead."

Ran groaned. Ship them where? In spite of great strides in space flight, locating habitable planets was another matter.

Leaving the plaza meant leaving the sunshine. Back in the shade he waved off biting gnats and rubbed his neck when one slipped beneath his coverall. The streets of Dodge formed a ravine of steep walls where no sun's rays could penetrate.

Two kids in blue school uniforms burst out between the first of the stepped arcologies, riding bikes. Clumsy things. Printed out by hardware fabricators. Ran itched to design something better—sleeker, speedier. Another kid in matching blue jeered down at his schoolmates from an airboard. Ran's lips twitched. He could even up that race by making that board move as slow or slower than those crappy bikes.

Sam's Antiques was on the ground floor of one of the oldest arcologies. But when Ran peeked in the window, the old man shook his head. Nothing for him to fix today. Disappointed, he turned away, only to step back to avoid bumping noses with a man in a glossy tan suit and unblemished face.

"You must be Mr. Kenelm," the man said in a smooth voice with a self-satisfied smile.

Ran took another step back. What a faker. "How d' you know my name?"

"You want a job, no?"

"What kind of job?" Free fixes? He wasn't about to be used by this Mr. Smooth.

Tapping his fingers together, the man said, "I could use someone to make the occasional mechanical adjustment. I understand from your coach at Eisenhower Secondary that you kept the school airboards in good shape."

Yes, he had. Mr. Smooth had that right. "So, have you talked to the employment office?"

The man pursed his lips. "No, I wouldn't say so. We have ways of getting around obstacles like EO regs."

Labor pirate. Ran shook his head. "I want a real job with real machines."

"The EO's already blacklisted you, haven't they?"

All because of a stupid supervisor. He could've cleared the jam in the trash compactor if the super hadn't shoved him away. Instead, trash had spewed all over. If he worked for a pirate, he could do what he loved . . . Except this guy acted like he already owned him.

"I'll have to think about it," Ran said slowly. "What's your name? How can I reach you?"

The pirate no longer smiled. Turning away, he said, "I'll be around. You don't have much time."

Ran stared after the man. "Blast!" He had to find work before they transported him north to that road crew. Hard labor. No machines. No future.

He'd thrown away his chances the day after he'd graduated from secondary school. The day his foster father, Doug, interrupted his repair of his foster mother's clothing scanner to ask, "Now what do you plan to do?"

Unthinking, he'd answered, "Start tertiary." The next level up. Of course. What almost every secondary graduate did.

"How? Did you submit your application?"

"Thought I'd do that today."

"Teacher recommendations?"

He'd stared down at his hands. His teachers had been too glad to see him go, the drag on their classes, the one who caused them all that extra work.

"I thought not," Doug said. "Two simple things you could have done months ago. I grant, you work hard. You graduated early. But with your handicap, you can't let up. No amount of fixes around here will take care of the other things you need to do."

Push, push, push! Even though he stood almost a head higher than Doug, the man made him feel like a little kid. He'd had enough.

"I did it on my own. I'll do the rest that way too." That same day he took himself to the employment office and moved into Workless.

But that labor pirate had talked to Coach.

Why hadn't he asked Coach for a recommendation? Except then he would have to face the other snag—his real obstacle.

With no repairs for Sam, the day stretched out before him. He walked for miles until, tired, he leaned against the blank north side of an arcology, soaking in the building's hum of ventilation and water recycling machinery.

"CURFEW BEGINS IN ONE HOUR," his implant announced. Oops. He broke into a trot passing beneath trees hanging over the streets from the arcologies' gardens.

Maybe he'd take that pirate's offer, he was sick of looking for stuff to fix.

Arcologies made way for municipal buildings.

"CURFEW BEGINS IN TEN MINUTES."

Better take a shortcut. With a deep breath, he cut through the last alley to reach Gunsmoke Street.

7

Two steps in, his neck hairs prickled—someone in the alley was wearing a cloaking device—but the soft whistle reassured him.

"Typhus? Another repair? I don't have time." Ran kept moving.

"No, we gots something for you." The young noid sounded excited, pleased. His shadowy hand came into view.

Ran paused to look. His breath caught. "A smart tool?"

"We owes you."

"I didn't do much." Only fixed Ty's vita-med fabricator.

The tool, shaped like a fat metallic pen, called to him. He flicked it on. Older model, still useful, humming with aliveness. Handy for diagnosing machine problems for Sam, or for Mukerji at Workless. Or Ty, if his fab went out again.

"Nice. Where'd it come from?" Ran asked.

"Swops clan said it fell off a garbage haul."

"Somebody must be looking for it then. No one would throw it away." Ran wanted it, badly, but noids lived by stealing.

"Swops clan said it were clean."

"FIVE MINUTES TO CURFEW," his implant announced.

No time left. "Thanks then. I've got to run before they close the doors."

He pocketed the smart tool and picked up speed through the alley, accompanied by Ty's cloak vibrations. Midway, he heard the distinctive growl of a high-powered Security vehicle as it settled on the street ahead. Another vehicle blew dust and stink through the alley to block the far end.

"Sludge and blast!" Ran walked forward on stiff legs to face two officers in black uniforms. One held a tracking device, face obscured by black helmet.

"You. Down. On your knees."

Ran knelt. Worshiping Security now. He risked a glance behind, seeing only blinding lights from the other end of the alley. Where was Typhus?

"Empty your pockets."

A setup. Thankless noid! Should've tossed that smart tool. Should've run back to Workless. Ran pulled out the smart tool and his little utility knife with its handy attachments.

"That's it," said the officer with the scanner. "Where'd you get it, kid?"

"It was just given to me."

"Likely story. We're taking you in."

"What for? Take the tool. And give me back my knife." He started to his feet. A baton cracked on his head. His ears rang.

"Get up when I say!"

"CURFEW IS NOW IN EFFECT."

He groaned. Workless was locked tight.

Hands jerked him to his feet and pushed him into the Security vehicle. He lost count of the number of arcologies they flew over.

In a claustrophobic room at Security headquarters, Ran found himself surrounded by hulking black uniforms.

"I don't know!" he protested. "I was told it came off a garbage haul. Use your brain scan. It'll show I'm telling the truth. And if you want to know where I've been, all you have to do is play back my records."

"Smart guy, huh? And any time you go down an alley, you have an excuse when we lose your trace. Sure. You're so bright you'd know how to use that tool, wouldn't you?"

Huh? Anyone could use a smart tool—

Oh. A smart tool could turn off the guidance systems of aircars so they could fly outside of controlled traffic lanes. That was what that labor pirate had wanted him for.

"And how many vehicles have you tampered with lately?"

"None! I haven't been near one. I haven't ridden in one."

"No need to ride. We have you on record as saying you can fix anything."

"I didn't turn any aircars into direfliers!" Ran's voice rose. "All I want is a job. All I want is to work with machines. I want legitimate work."

They didn't believe him. He was stuck here for a night or for a lifetime, whichever lasted longer.

"Lockup's crowded tonight," the guard said.

Ran found a seat where he could keep an eye on the other occupants. Street people, crazy but not violent. They didn't bathe much either.

A zombie shambled over. "Go away," Ran told him. At least, zombies did what they were told. Workless had them too.

Periodically shifting his legs, he used his fingernails to scrape gunk from the pitted plastic of his bench. One man slumped on the floor in the corner. Others slept or pretended to. Each time Ran's eyelids grew heavy, he startled upright, remembering where he was. He should never have left his foster family. He should have gotten a recommendation from Coach. He should have begun tertiary, even though he'd have to never miss a live class. All missed classes were replayed in virtual. And he couldn't. He simply couldn't use VR.

"You, Kenelm."

Sullen with fatigue, Ran looked up. Gray light penetrated the high windows.

"Yeah?"

"You get to go now."

Some of the sleepers stirred.

Ran dodged the zombie's arm and left the cell. His stomach rumbled. "What about food? You kept me overnight. I'm entitled to food and shelter."

"You had your shelter. Come on."

At the front desk a woman said, "Sign here and you're free to walk."

"Walk?" He lurched against the desk. "They flew me here."

His escort hauled him away from the desk. "Stand back."

He twisted out of the guard's grasp, addressing the woman, too tired and desperate for politeness. "It's miles back to Dodge Center. I have to walk back?" He had to get back to Workless or lose his things. Miles on an empty stomach.

"And what about food? No meal last night. I know my rights. Oh, *sludge and blast*. It's my work day. How'm I to get to the EO in time? You've really messed up my record!"

"*We* messed up? What about you?" said the guard.

"Give me back my knife."

"After you sign," said the woman calmly. "Won't hurt you to walk. Hey, Min, get the kid a breakfast ration." She gave Ran's thin frame a second look. "Make that two."

Out on the street a bus hovered past, throwing bits of grit. They could have given him a bus token. Then he'd have a chance at arriving on time. Miles later, the breakfast bars were scant memory. At the employment office, the clerk said, "Too late. You missed your crew. This goes on your record as a second warning. A third note and . . ."

"And what? I still have my rights."

"A third and you get checked in for treatment as an antisocial deviant." That veiled threat to turn him into a zombie wasn't likely. Courts re-gened only for violence, but after last night, he'd gladly hit something. Anything.

"You will work tomorrow to make up for today's lapse. And you need to show up for your regular day in line the day after, or you won't be registered for another week at Workless."

He hoped he still had a bed there after missing last night.

Food. Bed. He wanted both—badly. He'd be at Workless's door the minute it opened. Meanwhile, there was nothing for him to do but walk or hang out near a news outlet and listen to headlines.

Typhus—he'd believed the kid. And that labor pirate. The two had to be connected. Creating direfliers was exactly what pirates would have him doing.

The day dragged on and on. His feet ached; his head felt full of mush. He cut between two arcologies and angled up the street looking for the next cut-through to the older perpendicular buildings of City Center. A few more blocks. He'd be inside Workless the instant the door opened—

Someone on a bike sped into the alley up ahead. Not a fab bike . . . a really good bike.

From the alley came a yell, "Hey, stop! You can't—*uh!*"

Noids again. The bike rider was in trouble. Ran raced toward the alley.

12

Hallie

Hallie listened to her friend Cassandra's happy burbling as the train zipped along its rail toward Dodge, the city of Lawrence already miles behind them.

She was in tertiary. Their two weeks of orientation were over way too fast. She'd had such fun meeting classmates on that ancient campus, all wearing the indigo of tertiary students. It was unbelievable that years ago students had to pay for educations, but they had been so lucky to live away from home.

"At least I wasn't the only undecided one," Hallie said. The guidance counselor had suggested way too many choices: "If you should opt to transfer to the sciences, you will face extra class time to fulfill your requirements. Space science requires an additional year beyond that." No space sciences for her, even if her mother acted as if she came from another planet.

Cass's eyes glowed. "I don't know how I'll have time for everything. Lectures. Virtual labs. Once-a-month trips back for direct lab supervision. And the other students! I felt so at home with them."

Hallie envied her friends. First Vanessa off to Chicago for her music, and now Cass—unbearably excited about a future in the medical arts.

"Enough about me," said Cass. "Did you meet anyone special?"

"Mm . . ." said Hallie. "Miguel walked with me. He wants to be a tertiary lecturer."

"You have to have charisma for that, as well as be a great teacher," said Cass.

"He was good looking, but nothing like my history lecturer." She'd sighed along with half the class when Dr. Wing, of both Native American and Asian Indian ancestry, strode out onto the lecture stage, his straight, black hair smoothed into a tight queue. His white smile had beamed directly at her. "Dr. Wing made me want to be on time for all his classes."

Orientation had ended way too soon, and so did the train trip.

Bags in hand, Hallie followed her friend off the zip-train. They approached the first in the line of cabs waiting with its hatch open. Cass's home being closest, she ordered, "Sunflower Arcology."

"SUNFLOWER ARCOLOGY," confirmed the cab. The hatch gently closed and they rose to join the traffic flow.

Hallie sighed. "I wish Orientation could have gone on forever."

"I've got so much to learn before my first weekend lab session," Cass said. "I don't know how I'll have time for everything."

Hallie's smile took effort. "You're lucky you get to go back." Home was going to be lonely.

"I won't have any spare time when I go back." Cass's quick understanding would make her an excellent medic.

"Maybe not," Hallie said, "but you won't always be at home."

The cab dropped Cass off. "Tallgrass Prairie Arcology," Hallie ordered.

Even before the short hop ended, a feeling of oppression weighed her down. The apartment was particularly silent after all the chatter of those two weeks. She set her bag down in her tiny bedroom and went to see what Mom had programmed for supper.

Her mother was talking on her phone implant. "Here she is," her mother finished.

Hallie walked into her mother's hug.

"Dear, that was Mrs. Bright. She says she wishes you had told her you were to be gone. She would have delayed tryouts."

"Oh, I forgot. I meant to tell her I wouldn't have time for her play."

"You could make time. She still wants you for backup. After winning the Dalguti Prize last year, she has such hopes of you. The part is ideal for your looks and talents. And the whole idea of distance learning is that you can shape your studies around your own schedule."

Hallie grasped her braid, still dyed from the spring performance of *Iolanthe*. The top of her head had returned to dull tan, but she loved her colorful stripes. "I intend to stick to the live schedule," she announced.

"But you, of all people, need to be around others your own age."

"I will be. I am! All the kids I know are on the same schedule. How else can I see them except by sticking to my schedule?"

"But I know you. You won't be happy unless—"

"Mom! Let me run my own life! I'm going to finish tertiary asap."

"The arts guild is a perfect outlet for you and your talents."

"I'm not going to be an actor." She wanted to do something that mattered—like her sister Liz who managed the entire city of Dodge. Or like Mom's horticulture work, developing plants to thrive in arcologies. She was a second daughter—where one child was the rule. She had to be worthy of her place in the world. She needed time to discover where she fit in.

Hallie went to unpack.

At supper she spoke of the campus and the fun of meeting new kids, but when Mom returned to the arts guild subject, she jumped up and returned to her room. She'd decide for herself.

At her desk, screen raised to begin studying, she paused. Independence was what she wanted. "Legal Net."

"LEGAL NET."

"How do I establish independence?"

In the morning Hallie folded her bed into the wall, making space to utilize her desk. Legal Net had called the independence of a minor a *legal fiction* unless all criteria were met. Too bad.

Life with Mom this last year since her father's death had been . . . *heavy*. She'd done her best. Why couldn't Mom live her own life, instead of worrying about her second daughter?

Time for Dr. Wing's live class. She activated her desk.

An hour later, Hallie closed her screen and stretched. Dr. Wing made human history so interesting—and he put modern immigration into perspective with the past. It had been fun to participate in the discussion that followed. But now, by comparison, the apartment felt empty.

She got up and headed out. Fresh air, walk a couple of miles to blow out the cobwebs. She'd cross the skybridge to Sunflower, see if Cass could join her in a loop over to New Mumbai Arcology, across to New Bangladesh, and back to Tallgrass Prairie. Then she'd begin researching that paper for Dr. Wing: human migrations across the ages shaped a pattern . . .

Hallie sent a thought to activate her tooth phone. "Cass."

"CASS CAN'T TALK NOW," responded the phone.

Elevator doors opened and Hallie stepped out. Along the high north wall, privately owned aircars and one taxi awaited. The remainder of the roof was divided into gardens and walkways. Treetops crested the roofline from the stepped gardens below.

First the dogs. Hallie brushed past aromatic lavender and broke off a leaf of basil to chew. She entered the dog run, verified the cleaning bot was digesting their poop and that they had water. Then she crouched down to meet Starlight, a small, fluffy black mutt with white spots, while her other hand petted Chichi, a white chihuahua trying to burrow into her lap.

"Hallie, can you join us?"

Spamguts! She hadn't noticed the arts guild women clustered in the arboretum discussing their next project. She wasn't going to be stampeded into Shakespeare just because they'd won the Dalguti Prize last year for Gilbert and Sullivan.

Hallie waved. "I can't right now, Mrs. Bright."

She gently set Chichi down. "I'll be back," she promised and stepped onto the skybridge to walk the loop alone. Better than facing the arts guild.

Halfway across, realization hit. *Dodo! Make a note.* She switched to her phone's journal function to record: "If I want to be independent, I have to act like it. I have to tell Mrs. Bright for myself. It's time to stop depending on Mom to speak for me."

Trees leaned over the street below. A flapping banner caught her eye. An airboard, its rider's right arm and leg attached to the banner, approached and flew beneath the bridge.

Hallie blinked. Edge on, the banner was unreadable. The rider looked half asleep—graceful enough, but way too high. The banner must be advertising the coming airball tournament.

She resumed her walk. Finish tertiary in three years, if she pushed it. Then she'd really be independent. The bridge vibrated at the arrival of a large, noisy group behind her. Hallie increased her pace. *Why are you so antisocial?* she could hear her mother asking. "I'm not." she said aloud. "Maybe I just want my own friends." Talking to herself now. Not a good sign.

A faint, high-pitched scream, like a siren but from a human throat. The airboard rider had reversed course, but now she crouched on her board, banner twisted over on itself. Hallie could make out one word, *Kansas.* An airboard was such a little thing to balance on— even with toe guards—and this rider no longer had her feet in them. The board was aimed straight at the bridge. The flapping banner waved its words: Kansas for Kansans. The rider's eyes screamed as she mouthed, *Help me.*

Hallie pressed against the transparent side. "Get down. Go down. Go-go-go down!" she yelled. Why fly up here? Get safe on the ground.

The airboard and its rider slammed into the bridge.

Hallie stared, open mouthed. Airboards had redundancies: ward-offs to avert crashes; gyros to prevent tipping; antigrav to

18

prevent falling. Instead it had slammed into the bridge with a *B-O-O-M* that brought Hallie's teeth together with a snap. Pieces of board went tumbling through the air into the leafy sea below. The rider—

Hallie didn't look. She was running. Those last steps to the next arcology took an eon.

Panting, she grabbed the solid parapet. The group following was right on her heels, hiding the view of—

Her hand over her mouth, she moved only when the others tried to crowd past onto the rooftop.

"Body bomb. Another one of those suicides," said a balding man. "The bomb is wired to the ward-off. It signals when it gets close to a barrier, the bomb blows, and the board crashes into whatever."

How did he know? Body bomb. Body parts . . .

Not in Dodge! Dodge was safe. The whole world was safe. But those pleading eyes had been no suicide. Or were they? Maybe the woman hadn't wanted to hurt anyone else?

No, she didn't believe it. But if not suicide, then what?

A woman touched her. "Sit down. Swallow. That's right. Or you can put your head between your knees." The arm around Hallie's shoulders steadied her.

"I'm all right." Hallie's voice shook.

The balding man said, "They'll shut down the bridge for inspection. We need to find another way back. I'm calling a cab."

Hallie blinked at a familiar plump face with wrinkles and fluffy hair. One of her mother's cronies, what was her name?

An emergency vehicle descended out of view, siren blaring.

Hallie stood up as she shook off the woman's arm. "I'll go home by the ground. I can't—" She was afraid she'd cry. Or scream.

"A bit of shock. You shouldn't go alone. Bret!" The woman called to the balding man. "She wants to go down. A sudden fear of heights."

But Hallie had spotted the elevator. "No, that's all right. I'll call a friend."

She moved quickly toward it and slapped the call device. "Ground."

The door opened and she slid in. Her stomach lurched with the descent. "Cass." Stupid! Cass wasn't available.

The ground floor was empty and echoing, dim and shadowy in spite of its lighting. Boarded-up businesses: Pam's Bakery, closed; Riley Shoe Repair, up one floor; Buckley's Recycled Goods, up one floor. This was nothing like the bustling ground floor of her own building. Her steps sounded loud. Rattles, cracklings. Just the building talking.

It was an older arcology. Closer to City Center. Liz complained about lack of funds for maintenance inspections. People said the underground people moved up into anything left empty.

She stretched out her arm to force open the door, but its automatic function worked smoothly. With a sudden exhale of breath, she burst onto the shady street and headed toward the crowd of people. Safety in numbers. Except these were the curious, and they were blocking her most direct way home.

The bomb! She'd almost forgotten why she came down. She pushed forward anyway. She just wanted to go home. But Security were everywhere, ordering people away. Black uniforms gathered up the tattered banner and collected pieces of airboard. It shouldn't have crashed. Was anything safe?

The ambulance lifted. Liz could be proud of her emergency crews.

Liz! She'd be working and shouldn't be interrupted, but Hallie woke her phone. "Liz."

Liz's voice recognition clicked on. "I HEAR BY YOUR VOICE THAT YOU ARE DISTURBED. ONE MOMENT." Hallie waited, thankful for the priority given to family members.

"Hallie? What's up? I'm in conference with the mayor." Liz's husband, Jeb, also a city worker, often joked that his wife didn't hesitate to boss the mayor around.

"Can I see you later? I just saw"—Hallie took a ragged breath—"something horrible."

"Of course you can. *Hmm.* I'd suggest supper but I've got a council meeting tonight. Where are you now?"

"On the ground. A half mile from home."

"Grab transit and come to my office then. You'll have a wait, but I'll see you as soon as I get back."

A bus. Of course. "Thanks, Liz."

"That's what sisters are for."

She was lucky. Hardly anyone had siblings. Exceptions were twins and adoptions. Single kids complained of parental pressures. Because Liz was so much older, Hallie had been like another single, except that she felt guilty, like she had to do something big to deserve to live.

Kansas for Kansans, always complaining, accusing newcomers of stealing their land. Global movement of peoples was a given, accepted by every country. Just because Kansas was inland, away from flooding and north of the hottest zones, Kansas for Kansans wanted to cling to their own safety but deny it to others.

That bombing was too much. Something should be done about them.

Pel

Pel leaned his antique Shimano bike gently against the wall and settled the straps of his backpack on his shoulders. Dad stood in the doorway, his warm brown features registering disbelief and disapproval. "You just started tertiary."

"I'll keep up. I managed orientation during high harvest. I can do this." Harvest had been a sore point. Everyone else got to spend two weeks on campus, while *he*'d been stuck picking peaches and early apples along with the rest of the village. Virtual was no replacement for actually meeting the other students.

"I'll be back inside a month," he assured his father. Sooner, he hoped. He had to do this. During harvest he'd planned it all out.

"If what you call your 'mystery' *does* exist, you're laying yourself open to being disappeared yourself. Then what do I tell your mother . . . and myself?"

"It can't happen. I know my gambol's a gamble, but the NODE tracks us wherever we are. You won't lose me."

"It's not tracking you that I'm worrying about."

"I'll be okay. I'll arrange a lift back with the delivery van. Meanwhile, I'm going to sell my birthright for more data storage and do in-depth searching on the library's networks." Off-site memory was guaranteed safe, and his for life, but it was expensive and filled up too fast.

"Birthright." Dad snorted. "That bike is yours to do with as you choose, but your grandfather would be horrified to find out how you've used his yearly gifts of data storage."

"Why should he? Granddad's a scholar. What does anyone use data store for, if not research? And besides, Mom always says—"

"'A young man needs adventure,'" Dad finished. "Which is why you choose to leave while she's away."

Pel bit his lip. "Well, it's easier." He returned to the doorway to hug his father.

Back on his bike he passed village homes and the surrounding huge greenhouses that fed the nearby city. Select crews managed the daily gathering of garden vegetables, but the whole village was obligated to participate in major harvests. Soon Pel bounced and juddered along the rough highway that bordered the division between permaculture and open space. The other lane was slowly being buried; here and there broken bits of pavement jutted upward in dying gestures as grasses and shrubs struggled through.

A small herd of antelope lifted their heads and disappeared into the sage. Prairie dogs turned away from sunning themselves to look at him. Half the world's surface had been returned to the wild, allowing plant and animal migrations. Maps revealed vast rivers of now wild land running north-south, with here and there east-west connections like the one he paralleled. It had happened too late for way too many species, but generations later, people were still protesting loss of land ownership. Especially the People First Party with its local chapter, Kansas for Kansans.

Pel's village was composed mainly of farmers and prairie guardians, jobs passed down through their families. His own parents, both teachers, were relative newcomers. Ages ago, when the aquifer went dry, irrigation became impossible. Following a fierce struggle against intrusive species—thirsty trees and shrubs threatening to overwhelm the land—the prairie was finally becoming grassland again, able to soak up the rare downpours of rain. With stringent water recycling—and ten million more years, or another ice age—the Ogallala Aquifer might replenish itself.

A warning bark. Pel jerked his head. An isolated farmstead at the very edge of the last permacultured fields. *Uh-oh*—two large, tan, short-haired dogs.

He put on a burst of speed, yelling, "Not . . . lunch. Don't . . . munch . . ."

Fangs caught his pants. His legs pumped, his wheels swiveled from one side of the road to the other, barely missing potholes and deep cracks. Dust, grit, or an insect blew into his right eye. A mile down the road his eye dripped tears, his legs felt like rubber, his lungs ached, but the dogs had given up their chase. Pel wiped his face with his jacket sleeve and looked at his ragged pants leg. He'd dressed so carefully too!

Not so smart, right from the start. These dogs were only protecting their farm. What of the feral animals that roamed the city's outskirts? Now *there* was danger.

His legs shook. Sweat broke out. Turn back!

No. He had to find answers.

The sun emerged out of haze to glare hotly. A tall, ghostly shape on the horizon gradually revealed itself as an old concrete grain silo, lonely remnant of Kansas's long-ago grain fields. Pel sped past, concentrating on a steady restful stroke. A zip-train *whooshed* by on his right with its combined load of passengers and freight.

The road dipped, then rose again to reveal the tops of Dodge City's tall, stepped arcologies. The sun already stood much higher. Aircars, barely perceptible dots, following invisible prescribed lanes performed an aerial dance above the buildings.

He pulled off his helmet to wipe his brow, then reached for his water bottle and drank deeply. Drawing a breath, he muttered, "Pel, Pel, Pel, what are you doing? Turn around, go back. Try a new tack."

Back through those dogs? "I made my decision, I'm on a mission." He needed the larger Net. Letting out his breath, he returned the water bottle and pulled his helmet back on.

Almost there. Pel pedaled steadily forward, toward the city skyline.

A roadrunner chased a lizard across the road.

The stepped pyramids of the tall arcologies seemed to lean over Pel, due to trees branching out over the narrow street from each step. After passing two, he had to jog around the next. Because buildings were offset to break the wind, direction lost its meaning.

Finally, an old straight street with perpendicularly walled buildings told him he was getting close. Straddling his bike, he dug his com from a pocket.

"You lost?" The kid had a bright smile; he was dressed in rolled-up gray-green pants and a tattered shirt of no particular color.

"I was looking which way to turn for City Center," Pel said.

"Shortcut there." The boy waved an arm down the next block. "I'll show you." He trotted ahead. Pel tucked away his com and followed, pedaling slowly. "Turn right at the far end."

Pel faced a narrow passage between two tall buildings. "Thanks," he said, wrinkling his nose at the alley's stench. He pushed off, eager to get through it fast. A few feet in, his bike bucked. He flew over the handlebars onto his head. Feathery soft touches brushed him.

Pel rolled over and got to his feet, head whirling. Two shapes rushed away down the narrow alley, his bike between them.

"Hey. Stop!" They were stealing his bike, one of them the kid who'd given him directions.

Another guy dashed past him, shouting, "Drop it!"

Pel stumbled after, furious. Now there were three of them.

The bike fell with a muted clang on the filthy ground of the narrow alley. The first two disappeared. Pel blinked. Where had they gone? The third thief picked up the bike.

"That's mine!" Pel grabbed the handlebars, ready to fight.

"What were you doing in an alley?" This guy, thinner, slightly taller, certainly no older than Pel, sounded angry. "Stay out in the open where there are working scanners."

Out was exactly where Pel wanted to be. Out of the alley. Out of the city.

In the street, he breathed easier.

The other guy kept his distance, hands in pockets. "Your rear derailleur looks bent. Do you have any tools?"

"Hands off!" Pel glared.

"I'm not a noid." He held up open palms. "You don't have to worry about me."

"What's a noid?"

"Someone without a chip."

"Oh. *Noid*—no ID? I never heard that one. Avoid the noids. Don't get decoyed. I'm annoyed." An understatement. "No, that sounds too much like I'm a noid."

The other guy took another step back. "D' you always talk like that?"

Pel's face grew hot. "I guess—under stress. Who are you?"

"Ran Kenelm. Unemployed." He waved at his gray coverall. His lips twitched. "But not a noid."

"I'm Pel Teague. I stopped to check my com for directions and a kid—a noid?—told me to go through the alley and turn right." *Com.* He felt his pockets. "My com! *Frass!* Where is it?" He turned back toward the alley.

Unemployed Ran grabbed his arm. "It's gone. That's what they were really after. Noids keep the scanners broken in alleyways. Security doesn't bother to repair them anymore."

"How 'm I to—" call home, attend classes, get a ride back . . . "Dung, scat, guano, coprolites, shit! Frass! Frass! Frass! I should never have come."

"Why *did* you come?"

Pel shuttled his eyes between his damaged bike and Ran, whose gray eyes matched his coverall. "I had a plan. To sell the bike to an antiques dealer for data store and do some research before going back to the village. I promised to be home within a month, but how—"

He bit his lip. "Without my com, I've no way to keep up with tertiary. Or call home." He glanced at Ran's coverall. "I wanted to find the free housing."

"I'll help you sort out your bike, but you don't know what you're getting into. Go home now."

"I need the Net. The city library must provide more than Social Net and News Net to its users. And I want to sell the bike for memory. I'll take my chances."

"I know an antiques dealer." Ran's head tilted as if listening. "There's only an hour before curfew. Hurry."

Pel pushed the bike after his guide. Coms were expensive! The bike's value was nowhere near enough for a replacement.

They turned a corner. Pel's guide stopped outside a shabby glass door bearing the etched words: Antique Sam's Select Merchandise. An old man, small and erect, opened the door and stood there, blocking entry. "You. What you plan to break this time?"

Pel scowled. What now?

"What'd I ever break that wasn't already broken?" Ran was grinning. "I've brought you some business, Sam. Look, an antique."

Sam's eyes flashed between Pel and his bike. "You looking to sell?"

Pel nodded.

"Let's see it," said the man, opening the door wider. "You own it?"

Pel stiffened. "It's mine. My grandfather gave it to me. Titanium frame. I rode it to Dodge. Then, some . . . noids tried to steal it. It's damaged," he finished.

"It's only gears out of whack," said Ran, far too eagerly. "The rear derailleur. I'll fix it, but curfew warning's already sounded. I can come back tomorrow." His face fell. "No, the day after."

The man nodded and moved over to a desk. The room smelled of wax and oils, but held no visible stock. Sam and Ran dickered quickly.

"He's after data store, Sam. You know what that costs. And I'll be back to fix it—no charge!"

Sam laughed. "Trust you for that!" Turning to Pel, "I require certification that you are the rightful owner. Your hand print here. And a read off of your ID chip. The purchase price—upload of data storage to your Net account—when certification is confirmed."

A ping. The deal was sealed. Unemployed Ran and Antique Sam were laughing, talking.

What a fix up, mix-up, twist up. Pel ached. He followed Ran, bike bag on his shoulder bouncing against his pack, as they trotted through the open street. His left knee took fire, displacing shoulder pains.

At a darker corner Ran turned. "We're late and have to take a shortcut. Stay alert."

Pel jumped at every shadow, even having nothing of value left to steal. And he still distrusted this eager helper. "What's in it for you?"

Back in the wider street, Ran flashed a crooked grin. "I get to fix it, don't I? Machines are my field. I help Sam when I can."

"Oh. My forte's research—the reason I need data store." Pel ground his teeth together to silence his tongue, legs almost too heavy to move, knee throbbing. "Will they make me spend the night on the streets?"

"Nah. You've a day's grace—if we get there before the doors close. Listen, most of the men are decent, but some you don't want to trust." They slipped through double doors. A loudspeaker announced, "THE EATERY WILL CLOSE IN FIVE MINUTES."

Ran nodded toward a smiling, gray-haired East Asian. "A new one, Mukerji."

The doorman aimed a hand scanner at him. A mechanical voice read Pel's chip: "CONFIRMED. LOGGED. VISITOR HAS TWENTY-FOUR HOURS TO REGISTER. TWO MEALS, BED NUMBER 241 ASSIGNED. HAND

PRINT PLEASE." Pel placed his hand on the palm reader. He had a bed.

"I'll show him, Mukerji," said Ran. "Thanks." His gray eyes turned to Pel. "Eat first. Once you claim your bed, hang on to it. Unoccupied, they'll steal anything, pillow, covers, clothes . . ."

"Charming." He'd wait, imitate. But without his com—

The eatery was almost empty. A few men in gray were leaving as they entered. One stopped. "Ran, boy. Simpson was looking for you."

Ran shrugged. "I'm here." He picked up a tray and piled it with everything offered.

Pel followed suit, his stomach clamped to his backbone. Then his nose wrinkled. "What *is* this stuff?" He gingerly lowered himself onto a bench and shifted his bike bag and pack off his shoulder.

Ran was shoveling food in like he was starved. He swallowed and said, "From an industrial-sized food fab. Either it's better than it used to be or else I'm getting used to it."

"Glad I didn't come six months ago then," Pel muttered.

Ran bit into a roll. "I've survived a month on it."

A big man loomed over Ran's shoulder, holding out a com. "The young fixer. Here, boy, can you fix this?"

Ran held it a moment and shook his head. "It's dead. I repair. I don't perform miracles."

"I've been cheated! Those . . ."

Ran turned his back on the raging man.

"How did you know it was dead?" Pel asked.

"It's . . . like a vibration. I can't explain." Ran shrugged. "If they have any life to them, I can usually get them to work again."

Pel nodded, wondering again why Ran lived here. "You're attuned to smart machines. My bike's not smart."

"I like machines of any kind. They don't let you down." Ran got up. "Once the doors are closed, you can have seconds." He piled more food on his tray.

Pel hoped he never got that hungry. He tailed Ran up to the wide dormitory floor, walls lined with closed boxes, like Grandad's ancient Murphy bed, but these were self-propelled. A few beds were down, men lounging on them. Other men grouped around tables.

"Your palm print will lower your bed, but you want to be ready to claim it. There's an attached locker for your things," Ran instructed.

Pel's locker responded to his palm print. He threw his bags inside.

Ran yawned. "You play chess? I've got a set." At the other end of the long room, he pulled out a box from his own storage locker and brought down a table from the wall beside his bed.

Pel rolled a hand-carved pawn between his fingers. The rough cuts were plain to see, but someone had sanded it smooth. "Old fashioned!"

Ran's grin was lopsided. "Yeah."

"A machine guy with a nonelectronic chess set. Paradox reigns." Pel won the hard-fought game but could hardly keep his eyes open. Stifling a groan, he pulled himself up.

Ran looked equally tired. "Tomorrow I'll show you where to register. Laundry and showers through there." He nodded toward the obvious doors.

Brushing his teeth woke Pel enough to take in his surroundings. He met his own dark eyes in the mirror. No com. All he had left was a little dumb noter. He should go home, use the house screen, get on with tertiary.

His jacket had a filthy stain where he'd landed on his shoulder. He threw it into a quick-clean slot in the wall and stepped into the shower, which heated and comforted his bruises but shut off before he began to scrub.

"*And so to bed, barely fed. In my dirt, how I hurt*," he muttered.

He retrieved his jacket and approached number 241, applied his palm print, and climbed on the cot that descended, his relieved sigh almost a groan.

Pel's cot creaked. His eyes flew open. "Get off my bed!"

A dark shape shuffled away with a sniffle.

"No need to yell at a zombie," chided a voice out of the darkening room. "He'll go if you tell him."

Pel shivered. Zombies—violent criminals with their brains rewired. Bad food. Lost com. He lay back and shut his eyes, leg muscles still trying to pedal that bike. No longer his bike. Give it all up. Get a ride home in the morning. Let the village jeer at him.

el woke with a yelp.

The man in the next bed grunted, "*Huh?*"

Shaking, Pel sat up. Like the beginning of all his nightmares, he'd been running across the prairie, searching for Mik as a swirling purple mass of wind roared nearer and nearer. He turned to flee, then looked back. This time the tornado morphed into an enormous wave. The ocean crashed down, burying him under black depths of saltwater.

That settled it. He couldn't outrun his nightmares. He had to stay. Do the research. *Then* go home.

Mysteries

Ran

Ran sank into bed. No sleep last night. Missed work crew. Marks on his record. That labor pirate wasn't going to manipulate him. Not after that setup with the smart tool.

At first meal, he found two empty places and waited for Pel to dodge a zombie. "If you're in tertiary, why are you here?"

Pel stuck a fork into the gray mound of scramble on his plate. "Research. I'm here for the private networks. No one can afford them in the village. Dodge's public library has got to offer them. Why aren't you in tertiary?"

Ran grimaced. "I fought with my foster father. He was always telling me what to do and how to do it. And I should have listened. *Aargh!*" He scrubbed his hands through his short hair. "Why do you need private networks for tertiary classes?"

"I don't. Not for tertiary." Pel looked around. "Where are the unemployed females?"

Ran shrugged. "I've never seen any. Why are you putting yourself in line for unskilled labor if you're doing tertiary?"

Pel jumped to his feet, tray in hand.

Ran swallowed his bite. "Here, don't throw that away. I'll eat it." He speared the half-eaten roll with his fork.

Pel shoved his tray at Ran. "*Eww!* Have it. But"—his eyes bulged—"what d' you mean, in line for unskilled labor? I'm not in danger of being hired, am I? Look at you."

Ran shook his head. "They hire all the time, but someone blacklisted me. You're young, bright, strong. A good prospect."

Pel jumped up. "*Awk!* Oh, *grue!* What'll I do? I need time!"

Ran shrugged. "You'll have a few days, probably. For sure, you're stuck with reporting to the EO twice a week, once for your housing, and once to put in a day's labor to pay for it. Let's go." They dumped their trays, and he led the way through the streets. "So why'd you come?"

"I haven't a clue what you—"

"What are you afraid of?" Ran interrupted, "Nothing's secret anymore." What a weirdo.

The news box's volume rose as they passed it. "RECORD-BREAKING TICKET SALES FOR UPCOMING NATIONAL AIRBALL TOURNAMENT. ANOTHER SUICIDE BOMBING. TEMPESTUOUS CITY BUDGET HEARING."

In the quieter space beyond, Pel answered. "See, I couldn't keep quiet in the village. They felt threatened by my questions."

"I took you for loco yesterday. What questions?"

"It has to do with a mystery." Pel threw him a side-glance. "Disappearances, missing people."

"Here's the queue."

The men extended half a block. Pel groaned.

"I'm stuck here too," Ran added, "because I missed my regular day of work yesterday." To avoid questions about that, he rushed on, "What missing people?"

Pel looked at the building behind them. "Any ears?"

"Might be hard to filter all the noise."

Pel settled against the wall and muttered in Ran's ear, "Okay. The short version. While searching for a friend, I came across stories of other people who disappeared. Most of them could be explained away, but there's one particular period. One or two were whistleblowers. Others, I can't tell. But then, *poof!* they were gone. They totally disappeared. No information."

"No one disappears anymore," Ran argued. "Too well tracked."

"*I've got a little list,*" sang Pel before he turned serious again. "Really. Right before the NODE system went live. After that, no more missing. But during these certain few years—no trace. *Nada!*" He snapped his fingers.

"In our lifetimes?" Ran put all his disbelief in his question. "Martial law controlled street scanners, Net communications, traffic." Except for direfliers, mostly no one got away with anything.

They shuffled along the wall as the line moved. Others filled in behind them. After looking around, Pel's voice sank even lower. "That's what I'm here to verify. In the village I was limited to searching social and news nets. But here, after I register for my bed, and no job, please!"—he raised open palms to the sky—"I want to find the library."

"It's not far." Ran waved an arm. "Down Park Street. The library takes up one side of Boothill Plaza. You can't miss it. Or there's a guide on the corner."

35

"Wish I'd found one yesterday instead of pulling out my com."

Not quite believing Pel but his curiosity whetted, Ran said, "So people disappeared?"

"Gone without a trace. In the village, they said I was imagining things. And not to look."

Ran shook his head. "Are you sure about when all this took place?"

"I need to refine my data, but I think the installation of the NODE put a stop to whatever was going on."

"They finished moving the capital right before. There must have been a certain amount of chaos then." Ran grappled with the possibilities as they shifted to another bit of wall. "And the NODE—people are still resisting the idea of government by computer."

"Yeah, big time! Because the NODE is color-blind, unlike judges and juries."

Ran blinked at Pel's dark face. "The real power is wealth, not race. At least the NODE can block unfair convictions. Most interesting is they still haven't accessed all the information inside it. After fighting two wars to get control of that brain, no one really knows what data from Atlas Corporation were left behind."

"It's got to have the answers!" Pel's voice rose. "*That's* why I had to come, to dig up more facts."

Seeing transport arrive for work crews, Ran pushed away from his wall support. "That's me. I'll look for you at the library."

ifferent crew, same work. The boss kept Ran busy with trash collection—far from any power tools. Probably instructions from the higher-ups followed him around to each job, instructions like, "Kid is dangerous. Keep him away from machines." Protesting was useless.

They cleaned the stadium under a chilly, open sky, while out in the center, a school team played a practice round of airball, kids zooming around on their boards. Ran itched to get hold of one erratic airboard. It looked like its rider had overclocked the processor.

Tomorrow he could fix Pel's bike. But his days were dwindling. He had to figure out another approach to a job.

Pel

he men in gray slowly edged along the wall, ignoring Pel. Last night was the first time a nightmare had tried to drown him, as if telling him he had taken on more than he could swallow. And now the possibilities of being hired. He'd run home if they tried. But he needed the housing. What else hadn't he considered?

Across the street, a news outlet blared something about bombings. Bombings? Bombs didn't fit with those old disappearances. He'd stick to his own mystery.

Once inside, a bored clerk told Pel, "Report here every Wednesday. That means tomorrow. Your mandatory labor day is Friday. You show up every Wednesday for food and shelter permit, every Friday for work assignment. If after three months you remain unhired, you will be placed on a permanent, full-time work crew."

They could do all this with only one wait in line—stupid

duplication of effort. Collecting a gray coverall caused further delays. "You'll be questioned if you don't wear it," he was warned. At last his gray-clad body limped toward the library, clothes rolled under his arm. People following the sunshine milled about the plaza. Business types talked in groups; others stood at the transit stop across from the library.

On the near corner a man on a small platform held a Kansas for Kansans sign. "Don't bring them here. Send them off-world. We don't want those foreigners here." The speaker emphasized every statement with a thump of his sign's plastic handle.

Send them off-world—a convenient out, considering the huge expense of space travel and lack of livable planets. A body would have to be really desperate to go get zapped by alien bugs, weather, and other out-of-control conditions. The really gung-ho spacers were the explorers, xenogeologists, xenobotanists and xenozoologists.

Not for him. His mystery was on Earth, and so was his future education.

The library consisted of rooms labeled for various uses. He found the automated registrar in the main room, which was filled with tables and computer ports.

"YOU ARE PROVISIONAL RESIDENT ONLY. TWENTY-FOUR HOURS REQUIRED FOR CONFIRMATION."

Desperate, Pel went in search of a human. He had to call home.

The lone, middle-aged attendant was talking with an older woman with a young child. When they left, she confirmed the automated registrar's statement sympathetically, adding, "Meanwhile, you are welcome to explore the catalog of holdings."

Pel grimaced. "My com was stolen when I got here yesterday. My parents will be crazy with worry about me."

The attendant nodded. "I can override to give you one brief call to reassure them."

"That's a relief! What about private network subscriptions?"

"You'll find them listed, but inaccessible until your—"

"Yes, thank you," he nodded.

"The virtual collection is limited to what is freely available on the Net. But accessing even that must wait until your status is clear."

He shrugged. VR games, adventures, or stories couldn't compete with his info needs.

"Many people complain about our lack of variety," she went on, "but we're limited in funds. Subscriptions to private networks for research purposes get higher priority."

He grinned. "That's why I'm here."

Finally seated at a table with his privacy screen raised, Pel met his mother's worried eyes. "I'm fine! Someone stole my com, though, and I had to wait till I got to the library to contact you."

"You sold your bike?" his father asked over her shoulder.

"Yes. Got a good bit of data store for it."

"Keep in touch."

"See that you stay safe," said his mother.

"And miss out on all this adventure? Don't worry, I'll take care."

Pel closed their connection and buried his face in his hands. His reasons sounded so flimsy. Even Granddad, who had told him to face his fears, had looked doubtful when Pel spoke of his plans. "Wait till tertiary is over and you have the means to pursue this," he'd said.

But the nightmares kept happening. It always came down to Mik.

Mik's family had moved to the village when they were both ten. Their backyards adjoined; they'd done everything together—for that brief while. Mik, super bright, always talking of places he had lived with his greenhouse-builder parents. They had moved from one batch of refugees to the next, constructing greenhouses and teaching people ways to feed themselves while waiting for permanent settlement. Mik's dad always said, "Gotta feed the people, wherever we go."

One day while visiting in Mik's backyard, surrounded by his mom's herb pots, Mik said, "Before we came here, we lived near a camp of people. They got to live in tents. I had a friend there, Riga. Only one night her mom came looking for her. She thought Riga came to play with me. But she didn't. No one knew where she'd gone. I looked and looked for her. Riga's mom and dad went away and I never found out what happened to Riga."

"Let's look her up!" Pel said, proud of his ability with the family's com. They searched for Riga and her family. Deceased. All of them. Her whole family. Pel found it hard to meet Mik's eyes. He had wanted to set things right, but not like this.

Mik suddenly looked older. "Water warlords," Mik said. "They were always fighting."

And then Mik disappeared.

Their last day together hadn't been different from any other. They rode home from school, Pel on the smaller bike, still waiting to grow into Grandad's racing bike. Even so, he beat Mik by a nose and pulled up at Mik's door, laughing.

Mik's mom opened the door, and said, "Pel, you'll have to go home. I need Mikhail." He figured Mik had neglected his chores or something. The bike still lay by the front step the next morning. No one answered the door. The day after, a moving company packed up everything.

If it had been only Mik, he might have explained it away, but after searching for Riga's family, he'd realized *anyone* might disappear. And if he didn't watch out, Dodge and a work crew would swallow him whole and never spit him out.

Fastest way out of this town was through. Do the research. If he couldn't get started, he could get organized. Pel pulled out his little dumb noter and began to work out his search strategy.

✶ ✶ ✶ ✶ ✶

el yawned and replaced the book on its shelf. A whole day lost. There was only so much planning he could do before—

"ONE HOUR BEFORE CURFEW."

He jumped at the voice in his ear. His implant must have been activated by the employment office.

Ran appeared in his grimy coverall. Pel stood up and groaned at stiffened muscles. He picked up his roll of clothes.

Ran glanced through the window at the still figures in the Virtual Room. "Look at them. They say that virtual can act like a drug—in fact, they use it to get you off drugs, if you can afford drugs in the first place—but who's going to get you off VR?"

"You don't indulge then?" Pel said. They walked out into the open, traffic thrumming overhead. Across the square, a transit hover bus lowered itself to the ground with a hiss.

"I can't. I always break the processor."

"You what? That's some superpower. *Man*, how'd you get through school? All those virtual outings, experiments, museum tours . . ."

The bus rose. Dust devils blew grit in their faces.

"Gave my teachers fits. I read a lot."

Ran *had* to be bright to get through school without the virtual

41

education provided to everyone. Pel grinned. "Opiate of the masses, tool to gain a passive, submissive society."

Ran's crooked smile appeared. "And they got it. Now they blame VR for an unthinking workforce. I only wish I *had* work."

Stroking a nonexistent beard, Pel intoned, "Inside each of us is a resistance to change, and change is required if we are to arrive at where we want to be."

"Well, I want a job," said Ran. "And a horizon. Something far away—outer space by preference, but even open sky would do."

Pel's deep voice continued, "Horizons are in the mind, my child. You're looking for something you can't see and wishing for something you don't have."

"*Ha.*" Ran snorted. "I want a flight out of here, the farther the better."

Pel stroked his chin. "Now you're trying to escape yourself."

"Thank you for your opinion, Dr. Freudy. You're worth every credit I paid you. So how did you escape being hooked on virtual?"

"Research is in my blood. My grandfather's a researcher. My parents both teach. They use virtual in class but never at home. So you're not in tertiary because of your phobia? Can you call it a phobia if you break the processor?" Could one attend tertiary and never miss a live session? He already had a bunch of classes to catch up on. "I bet they have a translator to turn virtual into a flat recording, but you'd miss so much that way . . ."

Ran grimaced. "Chess after we eat? You won't skewer me again."

"Sure." Might as well enjoy tonight. Tomorrow, he had to stand in line again—*stupid system!*—and then work double-time on the Net. Classes and research both.

Hallie

Hallie woke in her tiny, familiar bedroom and triggered her phone's journal function to record. "A dream woke me up. Those eyes. They pleaded for help." She shut her own eyes. She was standing again on the skybridge, the woman's face distorted in terror, her eyes—

"Like they were telling me something. Liz told me it wasn't right for airboards to fly so high. Said I might have nightmares.

"When Mom and I watched the news report, they IDed the woman as some congressional secretary, called it a contract killing rather than a suicide. They said she wasn't the first, but they didn't even mention the banner.

"In the dream, I knew what was coming, but I couldn't wake up. Then that boom. And then all the pieces . . . But it's the eyes that I remember most." She paused.

"I need to think about something else. Why the Kansas for Kansans banner?"

Yesterday in Liz's office, she had asked, "Why don't they ban them? And why don't you stop them talking in the plaza all the time?"

"It's a way to blow off steam," Liz had answered. "We don't want to shut off free speech. People need a way to complain."

"But what if it's more? That woman who was bombed . . ."

Liz had said firmly. "We have no proof."

"The banner's not proof enough?"

Her sister had shaken her head. "It could just as easily be someone trying to frame them. Leave it to Security."

But now Hallie wondered what Liz really thought. She had remained silent, for an almost endless moment—and not thinking how to comfort her little sister. After all, Liz was in charge of the city. What if that group really was a threat?

Hallie's breath caught. Attacking a congressional secretary implied national concern. Some people said the Kansas for Kansans group was an off-shoot of the international People First movement. Both groups protested the division of land between wildlife and humans.

She resumed her journal entry. "Her scream. I can't stop hearing it. I don't want to go back to sleep. I'm going to find out why it happened."

Searches

Ran

In the morning, Ran rushed through dressing and eating. No second helpings this meal. He had finished by the time Pel got in line.

"See you tonight," Ran said as he dumped his tray and dashed off to be first at the EO.

After his employment office check-in, Ran retraced his steps down Park Street, past the plaza, heading for Sam's Antiques. From Typhus's alley came a familiar whistle. Big, dark eyes peered out at Ran, the first time he'd actually seen the kid. Ty had a thin face and ragged haircut.

"Fixer, you all right?" Typhus looked and sounded anxious.

"What do you want now? Whose idea was it to set me up?"

"Did they take the smart tool?"

"Yes, they took it! Said it had been used on a direflier job."

"What be a direflier?"

"An aircar, tampered with so it can go unlawful places." The ones flying them were also called direfliers, but why confuse the kid.

"I didn't know the smart tool were traced."

"Where did the tool come from?"

"I am going to find out. Clan still owes you."

"Forget it. Don't do me any more favors." Ran dodged an approaching food cart and took off at a run for the antique shop. He adjusted Pel's bike and left, Sam looking after him in surprise.

But at the sight of the labor pirate in his path, this time wearing a close-fitting silver suit, Ran's anger burned hot enough to melt metal.

"About our earlier conversation," the pirate said. "I have a small shop doing aircar repairs."

"Tell that to the EO." Ran dodged past him.

"*Hey!* I said I had a job for you."

"The answer is no." Ran kept moving. "You set me up."

"You're making a *big* mistake!" the pirate shouted.

Ran's trot became an all-out run. Mistake? Only one more on top of all his others.

His sandals weren't going to hold together at this pace. Smart tools. Ty's big eyes. He wasn't responsible for noids—but Typhus had cared enough to appear without his cloaking device. Maybe they'd both been used. Ran slowed to a fast walk.

Miles later, he had progressed beyond the arcologies. Warehouses loomed several stories high. Not much sky here either. Like City Center, these buildings went straight up, but he could smell the difference, a smoky, acrid odor telling of machine-driven work. His heart beat a solid rat-a-tat of anticipation. He should have come out here sooner.

Ran walked the long stretch of the first looming wall. Overhead, an airtruck descended. Loading and unloading were done—*oh sludge*—of course, on rooftops. With no street-level entries, he had no way to ask anyone about work.

He rested against a wall, soaking in warmth and the building's muted vibrations. Every mile he'd come had to be walked back again. Airtrucks growled overhead, accompanied by a lighter hum like a little Spark sportcar. Probably some boss coming in for a rooftop landing.

The hum grew louder. Too near the ground. Too loud. Ran turned. A Spark, all right, its transparent dome darkened. *Direflier.* Coming straight at him!

Ran dove for the corner.

"Hey!" a deep voice shouted. A heavy hand jerked Ran back, threw him to the ground.

He slammed on his side. The aircar scraped the wall with an almost deafening scream and zoomed away.

His rescuer, a husky man with a snub nose, got to his feet while shouting into a com. "Silver Harly Spark. Heading north, back into the north-south traffic lane . . . Yeah."

Ran sat up.

"You okay?" said the man. "You're young to have *malos* after you. What'd ya do?"

"Turned down a man about a job?" Crazy thought. No one would waste an aircar on him.

Ran got to his feet, one hand on the wall to steady himself, his head whirling, his blood thundering. "Someone must've lost control. Illegal, he didn't dare stick around."

"Next time, *cuidate la espalda*." The man turned back to his com, saying, "On my way."

Watch his back? Ran stared at the long groove on the wall. Neck high. He shuddered.

His rescuer was already out of sight. It was too late to ask about work.

The day more than half over, he headed back to City Center.

ver their game of chess, Ran told Pel about the attempted hit and run. "That man who rescued me told me to watch my back, but I still don't see . . ."

"Check," said Pel.

"*Awk*!" Ran castled out of check but, unable to concentrate, soon lost.

What was he going to do now? No way would he apologize to that labor pirate. Never. But what? His long slog back to Workless had brought him no new ideas.

is body slammed to the ground. A Harly Spark screeched against the wall. Ran's dream morphed into a voice saying, "You have to—"

He started awake. He had to what?

Sinking back into his dream, he used a fab at Antique Sam's to print out bikes like Pel's and handed the first one to Typhus, saying, "Tell it thanks."

When Ran got up, the men were already thudding down to the eatery. He stared at his food tray. What strange dreams. When he had first met Typhus, he told him to thank his machines. But he hadn't thanked his rescuer yesterday.

The smells out there, those big machines, the area called out to him. He wanted to go back. *Ha!* He had as much chance of getting a job out there as getting into tertiary. Hopeless.

He glanced at Pel, who was fiddling with his dumb device, a guy pursuing an impossible mystery. If Pel could do it, so could he.

Ran straightened. "I'm going back to try again." He wasn't likely to meet his rescuer again, but the big machines drew him. Then on Saturday, he'd track down Coach. Tertiary. *Ugh.* But Pel's idea of viewing flat tapes was far better than a life at Workless or in hard labor.

"Stay out of alleys," said Pel. "After that direflier yesterday, they might set noids on you next."

"They? I got in the way of somebody's distracted flying, that's all." Ran took his last bite of roll and stood, buoyant as if sitting on an antigrav engine. He had a plan.

Hallie

allie frowned at the screen. With a thought, she triggered her phone implant and said, "Liz, have you got time to talk?"

"A few minutes. What's on your mind, love?" Liz appeared, severe in a black and tan business outfit, though with a fond expression for her sister.

"Listen, Liz. The day after that congressman's secretary was bombed, he announced he was changing his position regarding the international embargo on planetary settlements. Someone is bombing people to—"

"Stop!" Liz's hand covered the screen. She lowered her hand and leaned closer. "It's possible, yes. We don't know. You *have* to leave it to the investigators."

"But Liz, they've got to be stopped. Someone is using threats and murders to get their own way with lawmakers."

"Love, I know that. Security has come to the same conclusions. Leave it. Concentrate on your classes and stay out of this."

"But who?"

"A person with a desire for more power than is good for anyone. Hallie, listen to me. What if someone used you to force me to do something bad for the city? Don't get involved. Leave it alone." The screen went blank.

Liz couldn't make her stop thinking. The bombing wasn't about Dodge at all. Liz wasn't in Congress, she had no votes on that planetary settlement matter. Besides, Liz could never be forced into anything.

Hallie shivered, remembering the panic in that victim's eyes. She had papers to write, but she had to get rid of that image of eyes.

She jumped up and ordered her favorite VR workout routine. Loud, heavy beat. Aerobic dance music. Other nonexistent bodies dancing along.

Sweaty and muscle-tired she programmed the food fab for supper and got back to work.

But when Mom got home, full of concerns for her social life, it was all Hallie could do to stay at the table. She wanted to make her own choices, in her own way.

As for Liz's orders not to investigate, she wasn't about to stop.

Pel

Pel began his day by running a search on Mik's full name and ID.

Nothing.

He sighed and logged on to his courses. Classes first, to not get farther behind than he already was. Much later, he switched to his list of missing persons, comparing dates of natural events—weather, plagues, virulent diseases—that might have triggered disappearances. He was missing something.

At the end of the day, Pel stepped out of the library into the plaza. Fewer people were out, though the ones he saw were dressed for evening. Unfair! Some people had no curfews.

The soapbox was occupied again.

"You folk are too young to remember. Everyone's too young to remember what it was like. Used to be, this was a little town, in the middle of prairie and cornfields. . ."

Yeah, yeah, ancient history, wasting the Ogallala Aquifer, burning carbon. This guy wanted to go backwards. The speaker—unshaven, three-day-old beard, maybe in his fifties—talked like he was two hundred years old. He didn't look poor, other than affecting a vest and boots like some old-time cowpoke.

"Took a long time to turn the prairie back again into grassland, and it's still more 'n half desert and sage now, no matter how hard we've tried."

On that point Pel agreed. He nodded, accidentally catching the man's eyes.

"But then they had to go sell off all that open land, turn it into prime real estate development for arcologies, one pyramid after another. What is Kansas now? A blighted United Nations, that's what!

Kansas has to house every last person flooded out of their homes! These intruders defile our sacred land with their beliefs and customs and languages."

Hogwash. Nowhere in the world was there a piece of higher ground without a mix of people taking refuge. The man had no empathy if he thought his sacred land was any more treasured than the lost, drowned places of the globe. Maybe he thought they should all be living on the floating cities instead.

Pel cut past the soapbox. Time to get back to Workless.

"Here, young fella." The speaker handed Pel a small card.

"Meet noon," read the card. What did that mean? Pel looked for the nearest recycle station to dispose of it. A tall, young man, with lighter skin than his own, straight black hair, and a straight nose, snatched the card and dashed away. "Hey!"

The speaker must not have known who to hand it to. Meet noon. Tomorrow? He should come out and see.

"CURFEW BEGINS IN TEN MINUTES." Pel pelted for Workless.

That alleyway shortcut loomed darkly, starkly; gloom, doom. He shouldn't have left the library so late. Breathing faster, he peered into shadows. One moved. He gave a shout and ran as derisive laughter followed him.

Back in the open street, he dashed the last long block to Workless.

At the last call to supper, Pel went in, wondering where Ran was. He forced down some food, scraped his leavings into the refuse maw, and headed up to the sleeping floor.

His bed lowered, he stared at the ceiling, trying to think about data, but his run through the alley kept intruding with fears, leers, jeers . . .

No Ran. No chess. He might as well sleep. Not much of that lately.

Gilbert and Sullivan lines ran through his head. "When you're lying awake with a dismal headache / And repose is taboo'd by anxiety . . ." He was no Lord Chancellor. He could describe his situation better . . .

> *While lying wakeful with a dismal head full*
> *of lost names you can't wrap your head around,*
> *with the least commonsense, you'd forego the nonsense*
> *of this life of bad food and lumpy beds you've found.*

Maybe he should consider becoming a playwright.
What a quark!

Changes Brewing

Ran

Urgency drove Ran, his sore hip a reminder of his near escape from that direflier. This time when the warehouses came into view, the traffic remained comfortably distant. The gouged wall was already filling in. His *neck* wouldn't have healed so easily.

"You again." The same man sauntered around the corner toward him, dressed in worn tan work clothes, a scanner in his hand.

Startled, Ran's heart gave a thump. "Me, again."

"They missed you last time. You came to give them another chance, mebbe?"

"Why waste a Spark on me?" Ran glanced at the gouged wall. "I wanted to thank you."

The man shrugged. "Guess I have protective instincts. Trajectory was plain as day. What brought you out here anyway?"

"Looking for work."

"Out here? What about the EO?"

"They've got me blacklisted. Machines are all I know. I can fix about anything."

"Any references?"

"References?"

"Anyone can speak for ya?"

"Sam the antique man can." *Ha!* A sentence worthy of Pel. "And Mukerji at Workless. And maybe Coach at Eisenhower Secondary."

"You said something yesterday about turning a man down for a job. Doesn't sound—"

"Labor pirate." Ran interrupted. "No security in that."

"What's a kid your age care about security?"

"I want a real job, not one creating direfliers."

"Like the one that almost got you. *Hmph.* Save a life, take on an obligation they say. Lemme get your ID." He aimed his scanner. "Not responding." He shook it. "Some glitch. Does this all the time."

"Can I see it?" Ran put out a hand, then pulled it back.

The older man cocked his head and shrugged. "All right. See what you can do."

Ran could see that the scanner was high quality, and it was humming with life. "Nice. Shouldn't fail to read." But the tool refused to show a readout. His knife wouldn't be of any use on this. "You wouldn't have a smart tool on you, would you?"

"No, but I know where to find one. Come on." They rounded the corner. Midway along the building, they entered an external freight elevator. "Five," said the man. The elevator rumbled upward and opened on a hall. Muted sounds of activity followed them into a brightly lit office cluttered with plastic flimsies and gear. On the wall, a wide screen displayed the building's exterior as well as the roof and street. The man searched through a drawer in a desk.

"Here it is." He handed Ran a late-model smart tool, big as a fat pen.

The smart tool sorted out the scanner. In almost no time Ran handed back both items. "All done."

"Well then, let's find out about you." The man aimed the scanner again.

Ran bit his lip at what his chip would reveal: lack of family, school records . . .

"Curious," the man said softly. "Not much here. So your name's Ran Kenelm? I'm Jeb. Jeb Talis. You want a job. You fixed my scanner; maybe I owe you, at that."

"It was *your* smart tool."

"Your chip reads you didn't show up for work on time this week."

Ran scowled. "I did a repair for someone. He gave me a smart tool—and Security was right there on top of me. They confiscated the tool and hauled me in for the night. They let me go in the morning, but they sure didn't fly me back—so I was too late for work crew."

"*Huh*. If they didn't hold you, they had nothing on you. I got an idea. Lemme check it out. And your references." He tugged his ear to indicate he'd be having a phone conversation.

A job! Ran turned to gaze at the screens, ignoring the inaudible conversation. No activity below on the street. A freight truck landed on the rooftop, dropped its load, and took off. Robots crawled out with a deliberate lack of haste to move the delivery. Robots would be fun. He would love to keep those babies in good—

"Here's the deal." Ran turned away from the screens to look at Jeb. "My wife's uncle is old. He restores antique furniture and needs a strong fella, someone careful."

"Family? *Uh-uh*." Every foster family he'd ever lived with had

56

disapproved of him. Working for one would be no different. "And I don't know anything about furniture."

"Job's temporary. Big backlog. You can give him a hand until it's through. Then we'll see what we can find that's more permanent. Better than the streets, isn't it?"

Ran chewed his lip. "You don't know me. Why should you offer me this?"

"You came back. Shows you're capable of gratitude. You fixed my scanner. Maybe *you* owe *me*. I saved your life."

"Maybe I'm a con."

Jeb laughed. "Your record would read different, I can tell ya. And Sam says not."

He needed to talk to Coach. He was running out of time. But a job was better than the streets. And if he worked hard— men at Workless had told him it was all about who you knew. Pel had taken chances, coming to Dodge.

"All right. I'll try it."

"Okay. Deal is—can't hire without legalities. So we put you in as an apprentice. You learn the basics of furniture repair. Not much future in it. But you're young."

"Do I get paid? Or is apprentice work the same as slave labor?"

"Nah, he's fair. He'll work out something."

Ran nodded, still unsure.

"Check it out. Go there now. You'll have to take transit." Ran caught the transit bit Jeb tossed. Then Jeb extended a hand. "My card. On the back's the transit code to get there. He lives way out—the other side of town, so don't dally. He'll be expecting ya."

✳ ✳ ✳ ✳ ✳

an swung off the bus without waiting for the automatic steps to lower. Gone were the tall arcologies. The city must have swallowed a village in its expansion. Protective walls edged the street, boxing in houses so that only rooftops were visible.

His knees shook. Things were coming together too fast, too easy. And not even a machine job. Sludge! He'd agreed too quickly. Sure, Jeb saved his life, but he knew nothing about the man. Maybe this was another setup.

He walked past single-family houses, all of them sheltered behind high, opaque fences. To judge by the barks and growls, every house was equipped with a canine alarm system. He double-checked the number on the card and looked for a button. No noise. Maybe they had a quiet dog.

A black tail hung down from the wall. The tail was attached to a black cat with an off-center white chin. Beside the cat's tail hung a cord. Ran tugged it. A mellow gong rang out somewhere.

He looked at the cat. "So announce me, why don't you?" The cat jumped down. A bar thumped and the gate creaked open.

"Need to oil this. We don't get much company at the front." A slender man with fly-away white hair gave him a quizzical look.

Ran said, "Jeb sent me," at the same time as the man's "Jeb sent you?"

They both broke off. The man grinned and held out his hand. "I'm John Sloan."

"*Uh*, Ran Kenelm, Mr. Sloan."

"Just John. Come in." They walked along a row of straggly plants on wire supports bearing green tomatoes. Other vegetables grew in raised beds.

The large workroom they entered ran the width of the house, windowed on both ends. Furniture cluttered the floor. Shelves against one wall held boxes, clocks, and unidentifiable objects.

"So much wood! And a fab too," as Ran spotted the boxy shape in a corner. A serious one, not limited to plastic printing.

"Yes, the fab comes in handy," said John. "That's my scrap heap over there. Furniture comes in chipped, broken, or with parts missing. Saves time to be able to fabricate precisely, especially when clocks need parts. You can see why I need help with this backlog."

"Yes sir," managed Ran. "But I . . ."

"You can learn—if you're willing? I understand you're a fixer."

"Yes sir," said Ran again. "It looks like . . . like you need some help." He might not know wood, but the fab—and the clocks—were exciting possibilities. He might prove useful here.

"Good." A side door opened, revealing a woman with streaks of gray in her dark hair. "Betty, this is the young man Jeb sent. Ran, my wife, Betty."

She smiled. "You'll have to save your tour for afterward, John. Lunch is ready. You'll join us, Ran? We delayed it when Jeb told us you were on your way."

"*Uh*, yes, thank you."

Cheese enchiladas. Ran discovered taste buds he didn't know he had. He looked at his empty plate. "Thank you. I didn't know food could taste so good. A friend told me the food at Workless is bad, but now I have something to compare it with."

Betty's face lit up. "You're welcome. I love feeding people, but mostly I lecture people on how to use their food fabs." She looked askance at her husband. "I wonder if I should look into the—"

"No," said John. "It's politics. Tell us about yourself, Ran.

According to Jeb, your references praise you as being talented with machines. He also said there was some note in your records about learning difficulties?"

Ran explained his VR phobia, and how he had compensated by reading.

"Self-taught, eh? Interesting, a meld of old-fashioned learning and new-age abilities."

His wife shook her head. "No matter how far we progress in education, there's always someone we fail."

The old man leaned forward. "And your weekly public service?"

"It's okay." Ran shrugged. "I work Mondays. Street and stadium cleaning. But I want a job with machines, and instead I'm facing a full-time gang assignment."

The couple exchanged glances. Then John got up. "Well, let's have the tour. I'll show you what you'll be doing. I'll show you your room. . ."

"My room?" Ran blurted. "You mean I'm staying here?"

"What did you think?"

"I could commute from Workless except on mandatory labor days. I thought . . . How can you trust a complete stranger in your own home?"

"I trust Jeb's report. Do you trust yourself?"

Ran's brain froze like Pel's out-of-sync derailleur. Trust himself? He didn't know.

At last, his thinking gears slipped back into place. "I guess so. I've had to. No one else is there for me, especially this last year."

"Well then. You saw. My need is great. Maybe you need us too."

What he needed was a permanent job.

But that left out tertiary. There he went again, putting repairs before long-term rewards. Exactly what his foster father always accused him of.

Pel

"Pel! You'll be late for breakfast."

Pel blinked and sat up. Ran stood over him, bag in hand.

"Where were you last night?"

"I've got work. Came back for my stuff." His eyes were bright. "I have to catch transit back."

"Back to what?" Pel burst out. "You haven't told me anything. What are you doing?"

"Fixing up old furniture. It's temporary. An old man and his wife. And the food—I'd almost work for what they feed me." He fished into a pocket. "Here's the address. Their name's Sloan. I've got to go."

Ran took a step toward the door, then turned. "Listen. Be careful on the streets."

"Yeah, yeah, Grandma. I'll watch for the big bad wolves." More reassuring, "Don't worry. I'll keep my eyes open."

"You'd better get up!" Ran dashed out the door.

Pel pulled on his coverall and picked up the plastic card he'd been given. Jeb Talis. No business name or address. Flipping it over, he read a scrawl:

John Sloan, Transit 105, transfer to Transit 56. 33,623 Juniper Street.

He tossed the card in his storage unit and sealed it.

Another thing he hadn't considered: the loneliness. "Who 'm I going to talk with now?" He checked for his little noter and headed downstairs. "Stick to your mission, stop wishin'. Ran's not the reason you came."

Funny, though, how Ran knew nothing of his family. Being a foster child shouldn't have wiped his records. Now there was a thought. What if the disappeareds he was researching had left children behind?

✳ ✳ ✳ ✳ ✳

Pel stood up. Time to investigate that "Meet noon" message on the card that someone grabbed from him. Would anyone be meeting on the plaza? A long shot for sure. If the message was in code, noon could mean anything, even midnight.

He blinked in the bright sun as he scanned the plaza. No one was orating, but behind the soapbox, the guy who grabbed the card was talking to another man.

The younger guy spotted Pel, and headed up the street. Pel took off in pursuit, down the next long block.

The guy turned toward a doorway. "Hey!" yelled Pel.

"What?"

"You grabbed that card from me yesterday. What was that all about?"

The snatcher eyed Pel up and down. His lips curled. "What's it to you, *zank*?"

Zank, the disease vector for the last plague. Pel stiffened. "Curiosity."

"Tough." The guy's eyes flicked at something behind Pel, and he entered the building.

Pel turned around. An older man with saggy jowls, the other half of the conversation by the soapbox, was tucking a scanner into his pocket.

How stupid. Ran had told him open streets were safe, but openness ran both ways. Now they had his ID, whoever they were. He'd made his bed. It was on his head. Nothing he could do to change things.

Pel returned to the library.

Hallie

Hallie looked at Liz through her com's viewscreen. "The bombings don't make any sense," she said. "You told me to leave off looking into them, but I wanted to learn more about that banner. Did you know Kansas for Kansans has speakers on the plaza soapbox every day? Why can't they be banned? All they do is spew hate and distrust. Just listen to them!"

She split her viewscreen in half to reveal the plaza scanner feed, with its current speaker.

Liz sighed. "Love, I see you're still trying to make sense of that bombing, but I'm asking you to stay out of it. Let Security run its own investigations." She rubbed her eyes. "Even though I'd rather visit with you, I've got to go listen to the city auditors. Enjoy your classes and your friends."

Liz was right. She wanted to make sense of that bombing. They had to be stopped.

Tertiary was proving less than heavenly. Hallie wished she had someone to talk to. After lectures, the students had such a limited time for Q and A. And she didn't have quite enough in common with her classmates to simply call to chat.

She wasn't shy. But they weren't Cass or Van either. Though their interests had diverged drastically, the three of them had stayed together. Maybe having something in common was less important than their long friendship.

Hallie woke her phone. "Cass."

"Hal, hi!"

"Listen, Cass, have you got time for a virtual jog or something? I'd love to visit."

"I know what you mean. I need to exercise and really, really have to book it or I get bogged down studying, and they say that's not healthy. Are you free tomorrow noon?"

"Noon's great. So a jog? I'll set it up."

Papers to write but . . . She returned to watching the noon crowd on the plaza. Public scanners were accessible to any viewer. It had been informative to discover what went on in the city. Now the soapbox was empty. The one who'd been speaking while she talked to Liz had quit. A good-looking fellow in a gray coverall came out of the library and approached the two men standing behind the soapbox. One of the men left. The one from the library ran after him and was quickly out of sight.

Hallie shut down her view of the plaza and got to work on her studies.

Mom was due home soon. Hallie closed her desk and went to prepare supper.

But Mom, when she arrived, had something on her mind. "Liz says you're thinking too much about that bombing. Maybe you should talk to someone, get your fears out in the open."

"I don't think so," Hallie said. "I just want to know why."

Heat rose to her face. "Is Liz spying on my search history? Has she decided I'm opening the wrong door in Bluebeard's castle?"

"I don't know what you're talking about. Liz didn't say anything about a search history. Now you're making me more worried."

Oops. Her mistake. "Anyway, I'm using my Kansas for Kansans research for a paper. A study of local people and their resistance to the status quo." A great idea! The perfect topic for her Human Migrations class when they got to the present day.

"Mrs. Bright and I are concerned because you're the only one your age in Tallgrass Prairie."

She could handle Mom, but Mrs. Bright meant the arts guild. If the whole arcology was involved, she'd never have any peace!

"Fine! I'll move to Aunt Bet's. Will that satisfy you?"

"Go, if that's how you feel about it. At least if you're with Betty, you'll be talking to someone, since you hardly talk to me."

"Mom, you're out every day. So is Aunt Bet. But what's good for me is good for you too. You won't have to worry about me. You could attend your grief group more often."

Her mother ought to be glad to be free of her second daughter.

Before packing, Hallie woke her desk and logged on to Legal Net. She was going to declare her independence, whether it was a legal fiction or not!

Atlas Corp

Pel

"LAST CALL. CLEAR THE DORMITORY."

Pel raised a groggy head. Not again! How did he sleep through everyone getting up? Simple, he stayed awake dreading nightmares. He slapped his palm against the bed's sensor to close it, pulled on his gray coverall, and splashed water on his face.

At the door, Mukerji gave him a concerned look but said nothing.

An unseasonably cold wind whipped through Pel. Should've grabbed his jacket. Smart cloth! It kept body heat in or out, but wind blew right through it. The city, with all its buildings, usually seemed impervious to weather, but today's drizzle teamed up with the wind.

Great Mullock. No breakfast. Cold. Wet. What was he doing? He couldn't think for lack of sleep. Useless, faceless, helpless, brainless. He shook his head. Stop that!

Shivering in line, Pel tried to focus on his search strategy. An old witness protection program had spirited families away to protect them, changing their names and identities. If someone exchanged chips and relocated, who'd know? But that rise in orphans and fosterlings . . . No, the old program had included entire families.

The line shuffled forward. His ideas dried up. He was tired. If they tried to hire him, he'd head back home, but he still needed time.

What he wouldn't give for some decent cornbread. Or tamales. Or sausages—as a vendor wheeled his cart past, wafting spicy sniffs. Pel clutched his stomach and tried to think. That first day, he had planned his questions. He still needed to answer: Who stood to profit from deleting the dissidents? Good phrase, *deleted dissidents.*

An annoying buzz drew his gaze to a helmeted airboard rider, dipping toward the line. It veered away with a second one in pursuit. *Buzzards.* They'd end up as airball stars or direfliers. Buzzards ate carrion. He was hungry enough to—

Down the line, Simpson yelled. His gray-clad arm swung up and out, lobbing a rock. Moments later, two Security vehicles descended and hauled Simpson away, as a wave of anxiety rippled through the men. The line surged ahead.

At last Pel entered the EO.

Back on the street, he tried to ignore his hunger. *To work, don't shirk.* Who was missing? Who would profit by their absences? Where was the common denominator?

Sam Suzuki had been about to interview who?—some military person—when he disappeared in that phony wreck. Gabe Fletcher, government accountant, had made one statement about the misuse of aid money and *poof!*, supposedly died of a sudden viral attack, but the actual details evaporated when examined closely. Geraldine Ramirez—something about monies for building arcologies . . .

Inside the library a line of unemployeds, driven in by the weather, waited for the Virtual Room. Pel grabbed his usual corner and sighed. First things first.

The lecture on human migrations. Pel brought up the screen and logged on. Classroom virtual was little more than a holographic display in his mind—nothing like the total immersion of virtual entertainment. Strange that Ran couldn't handle even that level of VR. Pel attached the library-provided contacts to his head; the lecture hall appeared with its sea of faces. There she was, the girl with the distinctive blue-and-green-striped braid. If only he had attended orientation in person, he would know her name.

Dr. Wing strode onstage, and Pel forced himself to pay attention.

Pel shoved the contacts from his forehead. That assignment was going to eat up all his research time. Too bad the migrations paper didn't include the recent history of dispossessed people moving again and again, fleeing wars, famine, disease, plagues of insects. He had a strong understanding of the period ending with the North American capital's move to Denver. But almost immediately thereafter began the Second Martial Law period, also known as the Computer War, to wrest final control of the NODE from Atlas's clutches. Atlas Corporation had then moved their enterprises into the asteroid belt, leaving the government to cope with the chaos below.

The curly hairs on the back of his neck straightened to attention—*Atlas*!

Atlas Corporation had been so big, so everywhere—like air, an amalgamation of government and corporate interests grown out of the military-industrial complex that began in the twentieth century. The final dismantling had required disentangling Atlas's financial tentacles from every segment of the global economy. There was the culprit.

No one else could have carried out such disappearances. Plan defined. Look for the mastermind. Track Atlas through its last thirty years. Follow the money. Not only government but also the Peace Forces had been full of Atlas appointees. So, he had to find out who was in charge during Atlas's final years.

He'd skip Comparative Lit class. Pel turned to the Net. The next-to-last head of Atlas:

> *Pierre Dalguti, president, CEO, chief stockholder, known as the "Kingpin," also as the Kingmaker. Dalguti admitted: "It's an aphrodisiac, a built-in hunger that can't be assuaged, an addiction to power."*

Pierre died before the final dissolution, control going to his son Auguste.

> *Auguste Dalguti, only son of Pierre, known for his death-bed pronouncement: "I'm entitled! My quadrillions paid for those ships and mine are the spoils. They won't get it."*

His many extrasolar scouting expeditions outnumbered all governmental attempts. The military had attempted to take over Atlas during the First Martial Law period, finally succeeding during the Second Martial Law era, which ended only fifteen years ago. Pel stopped to figure. Auguste died ten years ago. The time was right. And Auguste's descendants?

Etienne Dalguti, grandson of Pierre, only son of Auguste, sole direct heir to the Dalguti family trillions, gracefully accepted the loss of his family holdings during the final breakup of Atlas, claiming to prefer the little pleasures of life. He lives in Dodge City, his New Saudi Arcology apartment an antique collector's delight. Claiming he has no desire to be in the limelight, nor to have a target painted on his back, nor to have to answer to voters or Congress about his family history, he serves on the boards of several community charities.

The man lived right here in Dodge! Pel hunched his shoulders. Atlas was defunct. If the mastermind had been Auguste, he was dead now.

His next job of research would be to follow the money . . .

Ran

Warmth crept over Ran every time he entered the room the Sloans had given him. He couldn't remember when he'd last enjoyed uninterrupted privacy. His window overlooked an empty parking space. He'd never seen it occupied, but its beacon was live, permitting deliveries and visitors.

Downstairs, beyond the rectangular work space, curved walls glowed with soft color. The food and mealtime conversations could become addictive. All the same, he missed Pel. Surprising how fast they'd become friends. Was Pel's mystery of disappearances real or imagined?

The Sloans had provided a striped coverall for work, and tan street wear besides. But if this job didn't lead to something more permanent, he'd be assigned a gray coverall with the blue leg stripes of forced labor. That first day he'd blurted out to John and Betty, "I can't believe you'd take me in like this. The EO was always threatening to re-gene me as an antisocial deviant—and here you are, total strangers . . ."

"Not re-gene," John corrected. "They simply deprogram all genes relating to violence. A terrible travesty when you consider how much of who we are consists of choices—including the ability to protect personal safety and boundaries. All that wiped out."

"Yeah, we saw enough zombies at Workless," Ran said.

"Early parental care sets the genes you were given," Betty interrupted. "It's clear you received early nurture."

"You're saying that my mother loved me?"

"*Someone* did," said Betty. Somehow that felt right—like it might even have been true.

John nodded. "Epigenetic changes. Initial programming, simple when you're treated with love and care. You develop nonaggressive qualities, able to empathize with others."

Ran hadn't wondered about his parents in years. He got busy on the table he was sanding. The house's plumbing also mixed old with new. The shower unit was a water-recycling, self-contained model that he'd never seen before. He slowed his hands to ask about it.

John said, "Oh that. Yes. I lucked out. Surplus sales when they retired and dismantled that first Explorer spaceship. They shouldn't have done it—could have made it into a museum—but Atlas had no sense of history."

"Atlas Corporation?" Ran said incredulously. "But how could— did you work for them?"

"For one of their subsidiaries, yes. Working for them, you work with a limited number of coworkers on a limited scope project. You don't know what the big bosses are up to. That's a lot of years ago now."

John glanced up from the clock he was working on. "They called Atlas the 'Hold-Up' Corp. They certainly tried to hold up progress, but they're gone now." He chuckled. "They bought the Atlas name as a show of strength, not thinking how people would satirize the image of a man holding the world on his shoulders."

"Yes, I see what you mean." Ran went back to carefully sanding the grooves of the table leg. His hand slowed again. "Sir, I wonder if you . . . A friend of mine at Workless came to Dodge to investigate what he sees as a big mystery, regarding disappearances of people. I wonder if you are aware of any. Somewhere between ten and maybe twenty years ago."

"Atlas was just under discussion, and now this question. Are you seeing a connection?"

"Actually, I was thinking about Pel's mystery before we landed on the Atlas topic."

John looked at him over the lenses he wore for close work. "And yet, if there's anything to it, they were likely involved. I wonder if Jeb has any thoughts about it."

"Isn't Jeb a security guard?"

"Jeb? No, he works for the city's Infotech Department. They warehouse supplies and information."

Now that Ran thought about it, that building had been a city monitoring station.

"And Ran, we've got a two-week deadline on that table and chairs, so that's priority."

Ran got busy. Two weeks of good food guaranteed, then; bringing woodgrain alive, sanding pieces to satiny smoothness. Evenings, he'd already begun studying the books on clock repair. He was too comfortable.

He was putting off seeing Coach about a reference. Maybe coming here was a mistake.

L ate in the day Ran recognized the heavy thrum of a taxi. A neighbor. He continued sanding the chairback.

A girl's voice came from the car-park entrance. "Aunt Bet? Uncle Jack? I'm ba-a-ack!"

Footsteps came nearer. Ran looked up. His throat dried. He remembered her.

Tall with soft curves, the girl stood frozen in the doorway, gripping her single long braid, still in stripes of color from that production of *Iolanthe*. Her eyes flashed a lighter blue than her tertiary indigo pants and tunic.

"*Oh, spam!* Who're you? No, wait. Weren't you at Eisenhower?"

Ran nodded.

John came in and hugged the girl. "Hallie, we didn't expect you."

"I should have called. Mom and I disagreed over how I spend my spare time. I've come to stay. Is that all right?"

"Of course it is, dear," said her aunt, hugging her in turn. "You know you're always welcome. Ran is John's new apprentice."

John said, "Ran, here's our niece Haldis Pollard. Looks like she'll be staying while she studies."

"Hi." Ran wiped his hands on his coverall.

She didn't smile. "You live here?"

"He's in the back room, Sweetie," said her aunt. "You still have your own room. Come help me with supper, and tell me about your projects."

Ran turned the chair around and around again. He looked up. "What's she studying?"

"*Hmm*, general studies, I believe," said John. "She'll tell us at supper, no doubt."

The shepherd's pie and rolls were delicious. Hallie chattered about her plans to attend every lecture live. He'd *have* to attend every lecture live if he got into tertiary. He'd been an outcast in elementary and secondary, always the odd one, always having to study.

Tertiary wouldn't be any different.

Hallie

In the morning, Aunt Bet left to run a workshop. After Dr. Wing's lecture, Hallie called down to Uncle Jack that she'd be jogging and afterward would collect lunch from the fab.

"Oh? That means I'm to be cook today, does it?"

"It'll be delicious!" she said. "You love to cook." He might not be as good as Aunt Bet, but his choices were always more daring. Even Aunt Bet, who stuck to traditional tastes because of her years teaching people to program food fabricators to fit traditional diets for the greatest possible nutrition, enjoyed Uncle Jack's inventions. Hallie had noticed that Ran ate it all without complaint.

More cheerful, she settled in for her morning class. Later, she searched the Net for virtual jogging destinations and programmed a two-way excursion. She called Cassandra, pulled on her headband, waited for its contacts, and said, "Ready. Set. Go."

Their route took them on a trail along a small stream. Hills rose on all sides, cloudy sky with streaks of blue, grasses and wildflowers hugging the path. After a few minutes, they turned onto a dirt road that climbed the nearest hill. Stalks of grain, maybe wheat, waved at them from the right. Darker green legumes grew on the other side. Her smoothly running, virtual legs were sheathed in green. Though they could talk to each other, she and Cass saw only a single pair of virtual legs while enjoying the same countryside.

"Nice choice!" panted Cass. "Where are we?"

On the side of a hill, in the distance, was a farmhouse, a white barn, and a silo, and to their left a sagging building with gaps between boards. Old-fashioned buildings. The countryside was more lush than anything Kansas had produced in years. Hallie wondered if this land had been turned over to wildlife after that rush to record areas virtually when the ruling had divided the land.

"Um . . . 'The Palouse Country.' Northwest somewhere. Idaho, Washington, like that."

"So tell me about that lecturer-in-the-making that you were so excited about."

"Miguel's all right. I don't know. Seems like at a distance I don't feel quite the same."

"Pheromones." Hallie pictured her friend's habitual nod of comprehension as Cass continued. "Good thing to pay attention to. Maybe you were responding to that and not something more long lasting."

"I suppose. But it makes studies less . . . oh, appealing."

"You still don't have direction . . ."

"No, it's okay. But I had great hopes for making friends. I miss you guys, and I'm feeling lonely, a bit."

"I know what you mean. I miss you and Van too."

"At least you get back for labs every month."

"But they're all business. How are you doing with nightmares after that bombing you witnessed?"

"All right—mostly." They jogged up an incline, "Whoa! Nice view." Hill after rolling hill with a higher purplish rise beyond—but the program didn't allow for pauses. Their feet kept moving.

"Your nightmares? You said mostly." Cass wasn't about to let her change the subject.

"No more nightmares, but I wake up wondering why. Who would do such a thing? Horrible . . . because her eyes showed she was aware of what was happening to her and she was terrified."

"Well," said Cass, her breath coming now with faster puffs, "medical studies encourage looking holistically at causes—and they can be anything, physical, mental, emotional."

"That's what I'm trying to do, to find out why. Because of that banner attached to the woman, I've been watching the plaza and listening in on those Kansas for Kansans who take over the soapbox, but they don't make any sense. They're so inconsistent. I told Liz about it and she told me to leave it alone."

They had reached the bottom of the hill and started up the next long rise. An idea floated past Hallie that something must be *behind* that group. Who?

After several paces, Cass's panting voice said, "Difficult."

"Anyway," Hallie brushed that thought aside, "I've moved to Aunt Bet's. Mom was pushing me toward the arts guild's Shakespeare project."

"I can see why. You're a good actor. You have this way of *becoming* your characters."

"But how can I learn who *I* am if I'm always playing someone else? I want to get my schooling over. By then, I should know . . ."

"Oh, speaking of school, remember the kid at Eisenhower who couldn't do virtual? He's working for Uncle Jack right now. You know he's really smart, a year younger than us and already finished."

"Interesting. He'd make a great case study for someone working on phobias."

The blue and green of Hallie's quilted bed covering replaced the countryside.

"Good jogging route!" said Cass in her ear. "Let's do that again soon."

"Okay. Next time, your choice."

Hallie washed and went down for lunch. Uncle Jack and Ran were already back at work. Pulling her portion out of the food fab, she triggered her journal: "Went virtual jogging with Cass. We had a good talk. I told her about Ran's working for Uncle Jack, but that made me wonder why I've been so standoffish."

What had Uncle produced this time? Something spicy. Chiles, pasta, cheese . . . Yum.

Oh! She swallowed and recorded, "I didn't want to admit to my own selfishness. That's why his presence bothered me. I wanted Aunt and Uncle to myself."

Exercise had cleared her head at least. She'd be friendlier to Ran. Maybe even figure out how to get him into tertiary. A good project.

Worries

Pel

Pel stared into early morning dormitory darkness. Those two men on the plaza had IDed him. So what? Anyone could have done the same. He might have asked the man, "Where's my contact?" He gave a soft snort. Better that he didn't. Stick to his mystery and get out of town.

"I've got a little list," he sang under his breath on his way to the library. Little now, but it had originally been huge, from the Where's the Body? site. Most reported deaths were legit—plague and flu victims automatically cremated, landslide and flood victims not retrieved, monster tornadoes leaving pieces of people all over Texas.

He settled in his usual spot and brought up a screen. That question of fosterlings tantalized him. Match names of disappeareds against records of children. Sam Suzuki, well known for his virtual interviews; if he had a child it would be mentioned.

"Samuel Suzuki, noted journalist—"

Samuel Suzuki morphed into "Samuel Spitz, creator of popular virtual cartoons for children announced a new, humorous approach to interactive 4-D math, a breakthrough . . ."

Suzuki had been on the screen. Pel tried again. No Suzuki.

He switched over to Census Net. *Suzuki, Samuel* again morphed, this time into "Suzuki, Stanley."

"Awk." he whimpered. The Net was deleting stuff, playing games right under his nose.

If it could do this, it could also destroy his data store, remove it from the Net. No, not from the Net. From the NODE. *Panic, frantic, no, no, no!* Pel shuddered, struggling to remember. Yes. He'd locked down his data yesterday and hadn't opened it yet today.

At least his data were safe—and now he didn't dare go there.

> *What a quandary; sent through the laundry. A washout-out-out-out—*
> *Get out of here, into the air. Not fair! Not fair!*
> *What to do? In a stew. Can't think. Don't dare blink.*

What had set it off? Suzuki was on record, a public figure. The NODE couldn't deny the man's existence—*but it had!* The NODE wiping out an actual person?

Pel left the library, heading for Workless, but it was too early. He turned away, still on the edge of panic, paying no attention to his surroundings, still seeing those morphing words.

Pel's implant alerted him to the late hour.

He ran. Horrible meals were better than the alternative of nights on the streets with noids. A few blocks from Workless, he slowed but stayed in the open streets. No shortcuts today.

"*Wheeet!*" A whistle sounded as he passed the last alley.

Pel walked faster. No way was he going to turn in there!

Then a voice. "Hey you, friend of Fixer."

Fixer? Meaning Ran? Pel stared into the alley. Spotting a slight movement, he said belligerently, "What's it to you?"

A kid, dark hair and eyes, his faded clothing of no particular color, appeared seemingly out of the wall. "Fixer did us a favor. Aches clan doesn't forget. I got a message for you."

Pel leaned forward. "Aikes clan? Why should I trust you?"

"We owes Fixer. This be one way to pay him back."

"Pay him back? What'd he do?"

"Fixed our vita-med fab. You's friends, isn't you? Like a clan. You are the only one we's seen him with besides Sam. So your enemies is ours, see?"

A noid clan offering to be his ally? Skeptical, Pel wondered if he had enemies. There was that guy who'd scanned him. Or his NODE search?

He looked around. "How do you know I have enemies?"

"Free folks gets the jobs of tailing people. One of my clan, UncCharley, got the job of tailing you. My uncs agreed I could warn you, because you are a friend of Fixer."

Tailed? *Go home*, whined a little voice inside. But home was Workless for now. "I'm going to be late. I don't want to be locked out," Pel said.

"Come on through—safe passage. But I got to turn my cloak back on." The young noid disappeared.

Pel hesitated, but he wanted—no, he needed—to know more. "All right." He walked into the alley. "Your uncle Charley's watching me. Why?"

"Someone be paying Unc to watch you, be all," the noid said. "I don't know. Up to you to figure out the rest—but no harm from Aches clan, see?" The voice was barely above a whisper which Pel strained to hear over the sound of his own movements.

"How'd you know where to find me?"

"This be the alley closest to my clan. Go on now." They had already reached the alley's end.

"Thanks," Pel said. He broke into a run, his thoughts moving even faster. Why hadn't he asked the noid's name? He must be close to the mystery. Net, NODE, and noid, all standing against him. It was more than he'd ever bargained for.

Will I survive, come out alive?

If I'm in error, explain my terror any other way.

After barely squeezing through the eatery doors before they closed, he ate alone, his mind spinning. His fork scraped the bottom of his plate. Oh no. He was as bad as Ran, and still hungry.

Ran

At breakfast John said, "That large table and chairs, you've got two days to finish."

"I thought we had another week!" Ran said. "There's still a lot of coats of oil to put on."

"The owner's in a rush—and they take up too much space. Let's get it done and out of here. Maybe Hallie can help," said her uncle.

Ran caught Hallie's startled eyes. He'd been glad to not have to talk to her. No, he wanted to talk to her. No, she wouldn't hear him. No, he wanted . . . *Forget it!*

He finished eating and got busy on the fiddling work of chair rungs. But when Hallie came in holding the cat, his hands grew clumsy.

After a slight hesitation, she put the cat down and picked up a cloth. "I'll do that. You're taking off more finish than you're putting on. You do the big stuff." Corsair the cat nudged against Ran's leg and wandered off.

The table was easier than those little knobs. Ran tried to pay attention to his hands. It wasn't easy. Talk. Say something.

"You . . ." He cleared his throat. "You've done this before?" Brilliant.

"I've helped Uncle Jack, but I get bored and want to finish too fast. Then he tells me I'm not doing it right. *You* seem to have a lot of patience."

"It's peaceful." His hands got back into their rhythm. After a long quiet pause, he said, "When I was a kid, I used to visit a neighbor who carved. He always had a piece for me to polish and he talked to me. He was old." He took a deep breath. "He died."

"What do you do for fun?" Hallie asked.

"Work." He gave a shrug. "Beats having nothing to do. This is the best fun I've had in over a month, aside from a couple of chess games with Pel."

"Who's Pel?"

"A fellow who rode a bike to Dodge from his village. He's

investigating a mystery and pursuing tertiary at the same time. What do you do for fun?"

"My friends are all busy with tertiary too." Hallie made a face. "I do like learning to cook. Aunt Bet still lectures and does workshops but before, she used to work with companies on automated food production, how to get the best flavor and nutrition out of a machine."

"Wish she had charge of the food automation at Workless then."

"Why aren't you in tertiary? Uncle says you're plenty smart."

"It's not . . ." He paused. His tongue didn't want to work. How could he agree he was smart when he acted so dumb? "There'd be virtual," he said finally. His hands felt too big again.

"I remember that from school, but why can't you do virtual?"

People were always so disbelieving. "I panic in VR. Something in me shorts it out."

"So why not do tertiary all live instead?"

"That's what I'd like to do." He still needed to follow up on his plan to talk to Coach. "Do you know—"

Hallie politely grabbed her earlobe with thumb and first finger as she turned her head away to signal she was taking a call. "Hi, Mom." She walked away.

Lucky. She had a mother. *And* an aunt and uncle.

He needed to figure out how to get into tertiary. Betty Sloan might have ideas. But-but-but he had nowhere to live. Maybe Marge and Doug would have him back, or maybe he could live here and go on working to cover his housing.

But he wasn't family. He was loco to even consider it.

Pel

All night, words had floated before Pel's eyes, waking him up. Friday. His work day had come as a relief. He didn't have to face morphing Net entries. Now, raking leaves and picking up debris, those nighttime words floated up into his unquiet mind. He knew they hadn't been in his readings.

Whistlestop—he could only guess that it related to whistleblowing, but did it mean stopping the informers or stopping the abuse?

Thyme-sage—herbs, though why the words ran together he hadn't a clue.

Rosemary—name or herb? Rosemary for remembrance. All he knew was that it kept repeating in his head.

Crumbling pyramid—a warning or Atlas Corp's fear of dismantlement?

When work ended, the foreman called out names, including "Teague." Pel stifled a groan and stepped forward. The foreman said, "Recycling's looking for temporary hands, starting Monday. Are you men willing?"

If he said yes, research was out for the week. And without his com, there would be no time to view lectures during his off-hours. But Pel nodded.

"Report to the EO first thing Monday morning then."

That left only the weekend to check out those strange words and to catch up on classes.

Saturday Part One

Pel

On Saturday, bleary-eyed, Pel consumed his breakfast. At least he had gotten up in time. He ate it all, tempted to chew on his tray, but he had classes to catch up on.

At the library he slipped into the last available seat and called up a screen, but instead of tackling lectures, he requested "Whistlestop."

"A railroad term, short halt for fuel, water; early presidential campaigning tool . . ."

Patiently he moved forward chronologically through the search results and yawned . . . and yawned again. He rubbed his eyes, and jumped as "no link" flashed across the screen.

No link? Had he lost all connections? He backed out.

He was still connected. So much for Whistlestop. Try something innocuous. "Rosemary." Herb, qualities listed. Famous women, recipes—nothing more. No hint of his mystery, no names of his disappeareds there.

He took a deep breath and tried "Thyme-sage." More herbs, though why a compound words, he still had no idea. Recipes. FORBIDDEN ERROR flared.

Clearly he was on to something. Also clearly, *they* might be on to him.

YOUR SESSION HAS BEEN TERMINATED.

He reentered his password. Try something else.

PASSWORD DENIED. TWENTY-FOUR HOURS BEFORE YOU MAY REAPPLY.

Nowheresville. *His neck in a noose, fears on the loose. . .*

Big trouble now. No chance to catch up on lectures. At least he hadn't opened his data store. Slowly he shut the screen and stood up. He looked over library clientele; most seemed intent on their own business. That person in the corner—was he waiting or watching him? What did Uncle Charley look like?

He stared through the window at the occupants of the Virtual Room, their expressions ranging from laughter to grimaces to intent concentration. He was tempted to join them, shut off the world and wait in fear and unknowing.

Saturday was still young. He stepped out onto the plaza, mind racing, needing to move. As he walked an itch nudged at the back of his neck. If that was Uncle Charley watching him, he hadn't felt him before.

A directions kiosk up ahead. Pel aimed himself toward it. The street was empty.

At the kiosk he scanned the map. An airvan startled him. Only official vehicles landed on public streets. A woman in dark brown uniform climbed out and approached.

"I've done nothing wrong," Pel said before spotting the name Animal Welfare on the van.

"What, never?" the woman responded.

Relieved by her good humor, he sang back, "Well, hardly ever." Judging from her grin, she had enjoyed last year's countrywide Gilbert and Sullivan revival. He added in a normal tone, "Nothing illegal that I'm aware of."

"Well, fella, we're not arresting you. We were curious about who was walking this way. Didn't you hear our warnings? We've got a pack of coyotes to clear up and have warned people off the streets. Otherwise, you might get caught in the anesthetic spray."

"Nothing came through on my implant. So where can I go?"

"Where were you headed?"

He pointed at the map kiosk. "I wanted to find out where I am. Which way is Workless?"

She frowned at her own device and turned it so Pel could see. "You've come a long way. Our coyote pack is moving this way."

Pel looked at the surrounding stolid buildings. No admittance there. "I'm on foot, too slow to outrun them or your spray. Can't you give me a lift?"

She shook her head. "It's against regs."

"But what can I do? You were supposed to send out a warning and you didn't."

Her partner yelled impatiently from the airvan. She bit her lip in indecision.

"You're Public Safety, aren't you?" Pel persisted. "You can't just leave me stranded to be sprayed like one of your coyotes."

She shook her head, still looking at her device. "No telling which way they'll turn. All right, come on. Giving you a lift is the lesser of two evils, I guess." He followed her to the airvan. "You'll have to squeeze into the cargo area. We're not equipped for two-legged passengers."

Pel stuffed himself between tightly packed cages smelling of dog.

"We can't take riders," her partner said irritably. "You know regs have stiffened, what with the theft of all that spray."

"This one didn't hear the warning. Didn't you circulate the warn-off?"

"Of course!"

"To implants as well as buildings? Public safety is our first directive," she reminded him.

"I alerted buildings."

"And the implant channel?" she persisted. "We can ask the system."

"I thought I did." The woman's partner sounded defensive. "Picking up passengers diverts us from that same directive."

"So we let him off wherever we find the pack. Let's go!" The airvan rose with a jerk.

"They're on the run. Let's hope your 'Clear the streets' was signaled widely enough. Some of those animals are too damn smart. They always seem to know when we're coming."

"Who breeds these critters?" her partner grumped. "They keep on coming, just like the foreigners."

He'd be right at home on the plaza with the Kansas for Kansans speakers. Pel craned his neck to look down. They flew outside the traffic lanes, low to the ground. With wildlife and predators on the loose, walled-in neighborhoods now made sense to him.

"There they are," the woman said. The coyotes loped along, single file.

The spraying began. The animals staggered as the spray hit them.

A second crew was already gathering up drugged bodies when the Animal Welfare airvan landed.

"Sorry if we've taken you out of your way," his rescuer offered.

Pel shrugged. "Better than being carried off to be recycled."

She grinned agreement. "Recycle is spay, neuter, and relocate. You wouldn't like that either."

Pel distanced himself from the Animal Welfare workers. He was farther from Workless than before, drowning in his mystery and his pile of tertiary assignments and lectures. Time to swim somewhere, anywhere, and get his thoughts in order—if possible.

But first he needed to figure out where he was. Where was another map? He wasn't losted, but his feet were exhausted.

The kiosk Pel found was both discouraging and enlightening. *Here*, where he was, was much closer to where Ran was living than to Workless. Maybe Ran wouldn't want to see him, a fellow he'd known for only a couple of days. But he'd given him that card with the address. Pel located it on the map and memorized the route.

The buildings in the Sloans' neighborhood were single- and two-storied family houses long out of fashion, enclosed by high walls. Not so different from his village, but as an outsider, Pel felt more shut out by them than by the tall buildings of City Center.

He tried to shrug off a feeling that had nothing to do with Uncle Charley tailing him. Like he was *ambling, scrambling* through lanes of a rat maze, afraid of the NODE.

The next map kiosk blinked Out of Order. At a snuffling sound, Pel's head snapped around. Nothing. He was jumping at every little thing.

A soft whine. He peered under the kiosk. *A mop with a nose, it struck a fearful pose.* A tan and white long-haired dog crawled out, trembling but friendly.

"Afraid of Animal Welfare? Or you didn't want to be eaten by coyotes? You'd better go home. They've rounded up that pack by now. I've got to go find a place myself. You go home!"

The mop pattered close behind as Pel walked, considering his mystery. He was onto something solid, something almost within his grasp—but so elusive. Would he ever beat through that tangle of defenses?

Juniper Street. The house numbers were too high. He'd need to count down then.

The mop yelped and pressed against his leg. "I'd forgotten about you." Pel looked down, then followed the dog's brown eyes, which were focused behind them. He saw nothing.

"I don't want to carry a fleabag. Let me go. I'm almost there." The dog stuck close.

Scrabbling sounds from the wall beside him, a loud baying from the next yard. Domestic dogs. Were they barking at him or his canine follower, or both?

. . . 615, . . . 619, . . . 621. Here! 33623 Juniper.

Where was the button? He found a cord and yanked. A mellow gong sounded. No good. He needed an intercom.

"Yes?" a female voice spoke. Oh, good.

"I'm looking for Ran. My name's Pel Teague."

"He's not here." The click of the intercom felt quite final.

At his feet, the mop barked shrilly, hair all on end. Pel turned. The mop went on yelping hysterically. Pel's hair stood on end as well.

He yanked the cord again.

And again.

Hallie

Hallie's window overlooked the backyard shared with their block of houses.

A flash of red—next door's roses.

Movement—a dog romping with a child.

She wished she could go back to seeing the world as safe, like before.

The bombing meant someone was willing to murder people. For what? Opening up planets for settlement, cutting back on requirements, cancelling international standards. How could a national vote change an international agreement, unless persons unknown were also targeting other countries? Kansas for Kansans wanted to gain back control of state lands. This other entity wanted to claim lands not even on Earth.

Aunt Bet called up the stairs, "We're going out for a while." Perfect. With Ran and Jeb delivering the furniture, she wouldn't be disturbed during her favorite lecture. She settled deep into Professor Wing's enthralling description of Cossacks riding across the steppes of Asia.

The house com sounded.

She ignored it, but the house knew someone was home. Beep. Beep. Beep.

"Yes?" she answered shortly, willing her lecture to not fade out. A voice asked for Ran. "Ran's not here," she snapped. Keep the lecture going . . .

The lecture room brightened—

Beep. Beep. Beep. That com again! It wasn't going to let her ignore it.

91

Her room took shape around her, the lecture connection lost. *"Filthy spamguts!"*

Hallie stomped downstairs and out to the gate.

Ran

John Sloan inspected the table and chairs they had finished and polished. "Nice. They should be pleased. You can help Jeb deliver. He'll be by to pick them up."

"Yo, John!" Jeb's squat form appeared in the doorway dressed in the same tan work clothes he'd worn in the industrial sector. "So your apprentice is still with you?" This was Jeb who wasn't a security guard—this was Jeb the furniture deliverer.

"As you see. And as predicted, he's a fine worker."

They carried the table out the back entrance to the carpark. "An old Hefty Hauler! I thought I heard one." Ran looked with appreciation at the airtruck's small, rounded cab attached to a box-shaped container.

"Yep, they built them to last." They packed the table and chairs snugly into the truck's compartment. "Get in." To his autodrive Jeb said, "New Saudi Arcology," and the truck lifted off with a deep-throated hum.

Once at flight altitude, the truck swung around to bypass Dodge City Center. Ran looked down as they passed a green patch. "Is that a park?"

"Yep," said Jeb. "It's a nice one. Built around the neighborhood's water recycling plant. Trees, birds, pond."

"I've been wanting to ask," said Ran. "You saw my records. After

Security held me, why'd you trust me enough to give me this job?"

"When they kept you overnight? They knew you were telling the truth. Your records said as much."

"But Employment was going to hold it against me." His chest burned with the old unfairness. At least he wasn't there anymore.

Jeb flashed a sympathetic smile. The dashboard interrupted to announce "NEW SAUDI ARCOLOGY." He took over the controls. "Here we are."

They landed in the delivery zone on top of one of the newer buildings. Its northern side grew straight up from the street, allowing for elevator shafts. The other three sides rose in steps, each step planted in gardens. A dome covered the central part of the rooftop, protecting more gardens and walkways from weather.

Jeb spoke. "Etienne Dalguti."

A pause, then a voice said, "Yes?"

"This is Jeb Talis with delivery of table and chairs from Sloan for you."

"Ah, good. Follow the green lights."

A flicker of pale green lights appeared. They climbed out of the airtruck to unload. Jeb straightened the pad on the table. "Stack the chairs on top. We'll manage in one trip." He fastened a gravity-reduction device under the table, requiring only a gentle lift.

The lights led down a curved ramp to a freight elevator. Its walls turned opaque and they sank; moments later, they were in a curved hallway. Jeb and Ran followed the light trail to an open door.

"Come in." Mr. Dalguti wore the rich clothes of a penthouse dweller.

The wall beyond seemed entirely open to the outside; a thin screen of tree branches filtered the light. Ran forced his attention back to the table.

"Lovely." Dalguti lifted a chair off the stacked furniture as Jeb and Ran removed the others. Jeb detached the grav-reducer and pulled the cover from the table. The rich dark wood took on a new dignity in its move from Sloans' crowded room to this pale carpet.

Etienne Dalguti frowned and spoke. "House. Serapi rug design." A rectangular shape darkened beneath the table and began to fill with warm colors. An intricate pattern inched toward the center.

"Some things real, some things nano-imitation, eh?" he said with genial pleasure. "This table has been in my family for generations."

The carpet beneath the table gradually turned red, blue, and ivory.

Ran's eyes kept turning toward the windows. Jeb's nudge brought him back to the room and their departure. Once out of the elevator, they stepped onto the curved ramp leading to the rooftop; the ramp sensed their climb and pushed them upward. They emerged under the sky, high rises everywhere.

Ran said, "I always imagined these buildings had a horizon, but it's a horizon full of other buildings. Beautiful, yes, and a lot more sky than seen from the streets, but . . ."

"Horizons are what you make of them," Jeb said. "You expected a seascape maybe?"

"You sound like Pel. I want to look at a distance without buildings blocking my eye."

"Who's Pel?"

"Someone I knew at Workless. He biked in to City Center from his village to research a mystery."

In a few minutes they were beyond the arcologies and above neighborhoods of individual houses. "A lot of excited guard dogs below," Jeb said as they homed in on the Sloans' house.

"Who's that out front?"

The figure at the gate gave a loud yell and leaped high, waving his arms in the air.

"There's a cat—a *coug*ar. Stop it!" but it was Ran's hand that hit the control overriding the Hefty Hauler's course toward the back of the house. With a blast of noise, the truck jerked down below its altitude limit.

With a curse, Jeb knocked Ran's hand away, but the blast had startled the cougar out of its crouch. "Quick thinking," Jeb said. They bounced with the truck's self-correction.

Below them, Hallie opened the gate. The figure fell into the yard, his face turned upward as he staggered backward. Jeb was talking to Animal Welfare, even as the truck settled into the carpark behind the house.

"What's Pel doing here?" Ran wondered.

"The Pied Piper we saw is your friend?"

"Friend, yes. He didn't look like he was piping though."

"Interesting. I think I'll come inside with you."

Saturday Part Two

Pel

efore him crouched a cougar. *Threatening teeth on big padded feet.* The wall behind Pel was all too solid. He leaped high, waving his arms in an attempt to convince the cougar he was bigger than he really was. Landing, he fell back against the gate. Simultaneously several things happened:

Overhead, an airtruck sounded a loud *BLA-A-AT*.

The mop dog, half hiding between Pel's legs, panicked and dashed into the street.

The gate opened and Pel fell into the yard. "*Ooof*!" He landed on his hip and rolled away from whatever he had landed on.

A girl sprinted out through the gate, her striped braid swinging behind.

He recognized that braid! "Hey, wait!" Pel scrambled to his feet. "Stop! There's a cougar out there!" He dashed after her.

In the middle of the street, the girl whistled to the mop. The dog crouched down as she scooped it up.

"Dung, frass, crap, offal, muck, dreck, swill, feces, DUNG!" Pel waved his arms at the cougar.

The cougar resumed its forward creep. "Get back inside!" he yelled at the girl.

She turned, gazed at the cougar, and calmly approached him, the mop in her arms. "You, get in the yard." She ordered him as she jerked her head at the gate.

Step by step, Pel followed, never letting his eyes off the cat until the girl slammed the gate behind them both. Then he screeched, "What were you doing?"

"Saving your dog," she answered. "The cat was more interested in it than in you." She stroked the mop before setting it down. "You wouldn't have been much of a meal for that mean old cat, so maybe it did want to eat your friend instead."

"Not my dog. Both of us were cat bait. Any food in its craw, so long as it was raw—and available." Only the wall was between them and the street. "It can still jump!"

On his leg was a smear of red. Blood? *Crud.* No, tomato. He made a face and shook off the squashed fruit.

The girl bit her lip. "You'd better come in. Ran just got back."

He followed her down the walk and inside. He was finally going to learn her name, now that he'd acted such a yellow-bellied—

Ran rushed into the front room followed by a short stocky man. "Pel!" His eyes shone. "*Space.* To see you facing down a cougar."

"I didn't mean to drop in quite like this." Pel grimaced at his tomato-smeared coverall. "That was you in the truck? Thanks for running interference up there."

The other man said, "How ya doing, sister-in-law?"

The girl scowled. "Hello, Jeb."

"So you're in tertiary now. How time flies when a baby sister grows up."

"RESIDENTS ARE ADVISED TO STAY INDOORS. HOUSES ARE ORDERED TO FILTER ALL INCOMING AIR. WAIT FOR THE AIR CLEAR BEFORE EXITING," boomed the house intercom.

"That was fast," she said.

"Jeb called them," said Ran.

"Animal Welfare were already in the vicinity," Pel added. "They picked me up earlier for being in the way of some coyotes."

"When I was young," Jeb drawled, "that announcement would have been provocation for my cousin to shove me outside." General laughter greeted his statement. Even the beauty smiled.

Ran waved a hand. "Pel, this is Jeb Talis. I guess you met Hallie at the gate. And I see you ran into a tomato." His grin spoke of gladness to see him.

Hallie nodded like Pel was another squished tomato.

"Where are John and Betty?" Jeb asked her.

"They went visiting," said Hallie. "Neighbors. They'll be back after the air-clear notice."

In a low voice, Pel told Ran, "I need to talk to you."

"Come on. You can borrow my coverall until yours is cleaned. Stay for chowder." Ran looked at Hallie. "That would be all right, wouldn't it?"

"Why not?" she said. "Aunt Bet never turns down another mouth to feed. Excuse me, while I go finish my class." She picked up the dog and went up the stairs.

"*Uh-oh*," Pel muttered.

"We must've interrupted a lecture," Ran said. "Come on. You can shower and change while your clothes get cleaned."

Pel followed Ran up the stairs. Hallie had disappeared. *Lecture.* Of course. World Migrations. He was missing it too. In a tiny room, Ran held out a gray coverall, his matter-of-fact gesture clashing with everything Pel had gone through that day.

"I shouldn't have come here. I see it now. If I'm being tailed, I've led them here."

"Tailed?" Ran quirked an eyebrow.

"I met one of your noids," Pel said. "A young one. He called me friend of Fixer."

Ran stared. "Typhus? Why did he . . ."

Pel looked up. "*Typhus?* Is that his name? He told me you did them a favor once and they don't forget. He called you and me a clan. Said Uncle Charley was tailing me and I should watch my back, but not to fear anything from them."

"*Space.* I met him only twice, no—three times. When I asked how he knew me, he said his Unc Lum pointed me out as a fixer. Do you think they were watching me too?"

"Uncles Lum and Charley. A kid named for a disease. I bet Lum is short for lumbago. Aikes clan? No, *Aches* clan!" Pel gave a short chuckle. "Do they keep an eye on everybody?"

Ran's crooked grin reappeared. "That's really weird. Better get your shower."

Pel stepped into the warm spray. A rush of adrenalin caught up with him, shaking him so hard he had to lean against the shower wall. She could've been killed! He could've been killed!

The shower carried on through cycles of soap, rinse, and dry. Even after all the moisture had been sucked out of the tiny cubicle, he couldn't bring himself to move.

He tried to run the cycle again but it refused. *System recharging.* The story of his life.

Gradually he relaxed into something closer to normal, sighed, stood upright, and exited. He pulled on Ran's coverall, rolled up the sleeves, and tightened the pant cuffs, causing them to balloon slightly. *A brown clown, in meltdown, wearing a hand-me-down.*

Pel descended into commotion, the Sloans had returned. Introductions were mixed with chatter about Animal Welfare. Betty smiled warmly.

John's expression seemed equally friendly. "The man with the mystery?"

Pel looked sharply at Ran.

"*Oops,*" Ran said. "I guess I talked out of turn. We got to discussing Atlas, and I—"

"No, it's all right." Pel said. He was the intruder. He owed them that much.

"Will you join us for supper?" said Betty. "We love company."

Jeb ambled forward. "Then I'll consider myself invited as well. Your delivery fee will be amply remunerated by one of your meals."

"No Elzabet tonight?" Betty asked.

"Council meeting. She might miss your meal, but she won't miss me."

"It's her work, Jeb, and she's good at it," said Betty with concern.

"That's what I meant. She'll be too busy to miss me. I'm not complaining." Jeb turned his gaze on Pel, who felt like he'd been pinned to a board for dissection.

Hallie

Hallie returned to her room, holding the dog. "Come on, little one. You were in big trouble, weren't you?" A cougar in from the wild zones. They did that sometimes. The big cat had reminded her of little Corsair getting ready to pounce.

"Where did you come from?" she asked while rubbing the soft curly hair of its—her—ears. The dog wriggled to get down, then raced around, sniffing, searching for something familiar.

The lecture cycle was broken and she would have to start over. Doing all live lectures had probably been an impossible goal from the start. Fights with Mom and now this. She'd have to rethink her intentions.

Ran's friend Pel. *He* was the guy she saw while viewing through the plaza's camera!

"You wouldn't have been much of a meal for that mean old cat." She rummaged for Uncle's old scanner. "Let's find out who you belong to. I'll have to make up that lecture anyway."

She slipped downstairs to help Aunt Bet with chowder and to wait to hear from the dog's frantic owner.

Pel

The six of them filled the table to capacity, Ran and Jeb sitting opposite. Pel's every nerve was aware of Hallie beside him.

After his first mouthful of bean and vegetable chowder, he said, "This tastes like home."

101

From the head of the table, Betty smiled her pleasure. John asked the inevitable, "What's a fellow like you doing at Workless?"

Pel swallowed another mouthful. "I started tertiary a few weeks ago." Hallie started at that information. He turned to look at her. "I never got to orientation but I've seen you in some of my lectures." He dragged his attention back to the table in general.

"I particularly wanted to be in Lawrence to do some research, but the village needed harvesters. So once high harvest ended, I took off for Dodge. I planned to view classes in the evenings, not anticipating having my com stolen, nor the required work days."

John leaned toward Pel. "Why don't you go home? Finish tertiary. Your mystery can wait."

"Looks like I'll have to." The food in his stomach turned into hard lumps at that admission. "Some strange things have been going on, and today was the weirdest yet."

"First, tell us about this mystery," said Jeb. "Fill us in."

"So okay," Pel nodded. "Years ago I was searching for a friend and in the process came across lots of mysterious disappearances. So I decided to dig deeper. I managed to resolve some by comparing dates to epidemics and events, but a few fell into a particular pattern that I couldn't resolve. No actual death records, no explanatory events. A gifted cartoonist, a few who worked for companies connected with Atlas Corp, a couple may have been whistleblowers. For those, I reached a dead end."

He took a quick bite, noting Jeb's expressionless face. Well, of course, no one would believe him. "I keep finding new directions to follow, like Ran's being fostered."

Jeb threw Ran a side-glance. Ran said, "I'm not part of your mystery."

Pel gave a little shrug. "Well, you got me curious, because you didn't have any background. You fall within the right years. And when I looked I found a tiny uptick in number of orphans due to no apparent cause. Until maturity, specific information is private. But . . ."

After Ran's close call with the direflier, Pel wished he didn't have such a vivid imagination. He took a deep breath and continued, "I found news items on two former foster kids who reached legal age last year. They're both dead. One in a wreck that shouldn't've happened. His aircar was fully functional and should have evaded the direflier that hit him—so why didn't it? The direflier got away. Unsolved.

"Ran had a close call too, even though he's nowhere near eighteen."

He'd caught Ran's attention all right. All eyes were riveted on Pel.

"The other death was equally mysterious—a girl dead from some virus previously unknown in this hemisphere, and she hadn't traveled anywhere."

Pel set down his spoon and glanced at each listener around the table. "Now for the really weird stuff. I tried from the other end to see if any of my disappeared had kids. That first name I tried morphed into another, similar name. It happened again on a different Net altogether. The same name! And you can't tell me Sam Suzuki didn't exist and that he didn't make vids."

Betty said, "We used to watch those. A great interviewer before he died."

"Except he's one of my disappeareds. His crash is on record, but with no follow-up info on his body." That brought him to the next bit. Go ahead, prove to them he was crazy.

"That night I had a hard time sleeping. Whenever I woke, I could see words—nothing that I'd been reading. Words like *rosemary* and *whistlestop*. As if my brain had picked up on something subliminal—and only in the night could it catch my attention. So . . ."

He stopped for a sip of water. All eyes were on him. "So yesterday I had to work, and then this morning I checked those words. *Whistlestop* ended up with No Link.

"I reconnected and checked a couple more words. And then the Net flat-out denied me—took away my password—told me to wait twenty-four hours to reapply.

"I didn't know what to do. If the Net or the NODE can mess with my terminal, it can also wipe out my data store. I haven't dared open it. I've got assignments stashed there. How can I retrieve them without risking everything being contaminated?" His voice shook. He stopped.

Across the table, Ran seemed lost in thought.

"So what's this time period?" Jeb asked.

Betty broke in. "Enough for now. Let him eat. You can talk after."

Pel reached for his spoon and another slice of the chewy brown bread, listening to the silence.

After long moments, Jeb said, "You raise the disturbing specter of the NODE acting capriciously. Its brain was bred to withstand cyberattacks."

Pel swallowed and jumped back in. "I keep wondering. This funny stuff began after I looked into Atlas. But *if* they're subliminal words, *why*? Could the NODE *want* to divulge info and be feeding me passwords? But then why dump me out?"

"What if there are hidden files?" Ran asked. Jeb and John were shaking their heads. "Atlas stole the supercomputer," Ran defended.

"They didn't steal it," argued Jeb. "They developed it under government mandate."

"And didn't want to give it back while using it for their space explorations."

Jeb nodded. "True enough."

"The morphing has to come from the NODE," Ran continued, his brow creased. "Constant inflow of data, lots of duplication. Little bits or major bits might sit in a file until something triggers a response. Maybe one part wants to hand over a piece of data, and another part pulls it back?"

Pel disagreed. "That might explain No Link, but morphing words is plain crazy!"

"So when did these disappearances begin?" said Jeb.

"The earliest definitive ones date from the end of Second Martial Law and continue until the time of the J'burg flu epidemic. Some of my data are suspect there. Say, maybe from twenty years until about twelve years ago, when the NODE was initiated into government use."

"That's not long past the thought police," said John. "Older folk remember it only too well."

Betty nodded. "The reason we have such a conservative population these days."

"Tell me about it!" groaned Pel. "Villagers are even more cautious."

"Well, you didn't have to live through it. Your parents would have grown up with it," she said. "As if anyone can control people's thoughts."

Thoughts! Pel did a reset. Villagers had feared him and his mystery like a disease.

"Okay," Jeb broke in. He pushed away his dishes. "Thank you, Betty. Delicious as always." He tapped his fingers together. "I have many doubts as to the validity of your research, but in the interests of getting you back home, I'd like to share it with my boss."

"Who's your boss?" Pel asked cautiously.

"Jeb is married to our niece, who happens to be the city manager," said Betty.

Elzabet Pollard-Talis. Pel did a double-take around the table.

"I'm also thinking," said Jeb, "that she might give permission for you to access the NODE directly, through the city's infoline. You've been working only with Net sources?"

Pel nodded.

Hallie spoke for the first time. "During orientation one of my professors spoke of Atlas's targeting journalists and whistleblowers— until their own people rebelled. Maybe they're still trying."

"It always comes back to Atlas," Pel agreed, his heart thumping at Jeb's suggestion that he ask the NODE directly. "But what about my data store?"

Jeb gave a nod. "You're wise not to open it until this other issue is dealt with. What happens if you don't return to Workless tonight?"

A chill ran through Pel.

Ran answered, "One night, they don't pay any attention. More than that and your bed and belongings revert to their control. They don't go searching." A hint of bitterness in his voice. "No one cares enough—but they have a clear record of your absence if anyone reports you missing."

Betty echoed Pel's thoughts. "His family would care."

"That's right. If you prefer, I can drop you off at Workless tonight." Jeb stood up.

This far from City Center, Pel hadn't heard any curfew warnings. "I think it's too late."

"All the better," said Jeb. "You'll be easier for me to reach if you spend the night here. I'll report back in the morning. Take these"—he handed Pel some bus tokens—"to get back to Workless tomorrow. But please don't leave before I call."

"*Brill!*" Pel grinned. Transport, plus a direct chance at the NODE? What luck!

Hallie

Preparing for bed, Hallie woke her journal to record. "Imagine! He's in tertiary with me. And I almost got him killed! I was in the middle of Dr. Wing's lecture when the bell rang. I thought I could just send him away without losing my connection. But he kept ringing. And ringing.

"So I went down and opened the gate. Pel fell inside and a dog yelped. I ran out to rescue this little dog, and Pel rushed out, yelling, to guard us from a hungry cougar until I could get back with the puppy. He acted so brave—and he was so scared.

"I hate lectures on virtual. I'll have to start at the beginning again and miss the discussion. But I'm doubly furious that I almost got Pel mauled. *He's* the guy I saw on the plaza last week! I want to ask him about that. I've never even noticed him in my classes—all because he wasn't at orientation.

"I thought all I had to do was concentrate on studying, figure out what I want to be, and I'd be grown up. And now it's gotten so complicated.

"If he hadn't kept pulling the cord, he might've been eaten. He's got a great smile, he's smart, he knows what he wants and goes for it.

Everyone took him seriously at dinner, and all I could say was one stupid sentence, as if my tongue were tied in knots. Just one stupid sentence!

"I don't see how his disappearances relate to my bombing, but I can't wait to really talk to him."

PART TWO

FRIENDS

Spider poured himself a cup of coffee. A voice sounded in his ear, "Sir, I—"

"Tech. You're early." Spider strolled over to look out his floor-to-ceiling window.

"The NODE reported some odd search topics," Tech said. "It tracks to here in the city."

"The source?"

"A kid—not one of yours. He's getting way too close, naming names. And yesterday the Brain shut him out."

"If he's shut out, what more is needed?"

"There's a bigger problem. The NODE doesn't like keeping secrets."

"The Brain is your job. Meanwhile, looks like I'll have to get rid of this kid. I want to know everything he does. I want to know everyone he's associated with."

Spider looked out over his city and closed their phone connection with a thought. A pity he hadn't gotten any use out of that machine-talented kid. Too independent. They'd had trouble with the kid's father too.

He'd have to call on those Peacers to snare both kids. His Peacers didn't have much time left before deployment. They'd better not mess up again.

His lips twitched. Beautiful irony in that name, Peacers.

Sunday

Pel

On the floor of Ran's little room, Pel yawned and stretched. He'd slept, finally slept. Not even a nightmare of being swallowed by cougars. Ran had already gotten up. Hungry, Pel pulled on his cleaned coverall. A few minutes later, as he was eating breakfast, Jeb's voice came in over the speaker, asking for him.

"He's right here," said Betty. "Go ahead, Jeb."

"The city manager has signed her approval. You'll go through the Infotech Department head Esquivel y Turner. He's willing to see you next Saturday. That work for you?"

Next Saturday. He'd get behinder and behinder in classwork. But he'd agreed to work next week. "Yes, thank you," said Pel. "Saturday. Where? What time?"

"The Plaza Coffee Bar, opposite the library. As soon as they let you out of Workless. Bring the question you want to ask the NODE."

The instructions hit Pel with a jolt. A question. "Can I ask more than one?"

"That's up to Turner. Try your best to be direct and concise."

"Will do." The question would be crucial. How to phrase it?

Hallie

Hallie wiped the table, ears stretched to hear the workroom talk.

"Where's Hallie?" Ran asked. Aha. Her cue. Enter stage right.

"You wanted me?" she asked from the kitchen doorway.

"Yeah. When Jeb and I took that delivery yesterday, we flew over a park. Do you know how to find it? I'm walking Pel to the transit stop."

"Sure. I can take you if we go now. Then I've got a makeup lecture and lots of assignments. The park's nice, our wastewater purification plantation."

She'd had so many questions to ask Pel, but once in their company her thoughts dried up.

At the gate Pel looked around cautiously. "It's safe," she assured him. "No dogs barking."

"Good. We've never had a cougar venture into my village." They stepped out into the street and Pel asked, "What's your subject area?"

"Undecided," she admitted. "Yours?"

"Same, but definitely to do with research."

For a few blocks they discussed their assigned Human Migrations papers, until Hallie announced, "Here we are." She turned between two houses, led them through a disguised gate and down a passage to reveal a long patch of green, with scattered shade trees. "A jogging path circles the edge, and there's a pond hidden down there." She led them through a screen of trees toward the water. "My favorite spot." She waved at a little arched bridge.

Pel followed her onto the bridge while Ran wandered down to the pond.

Now was her chance. "I've got a mystery of my own," she began, and told Pel of the bombing. "I started watching the plaza's soapbox and I'm sure I saw you there one day. You approached a couple men and then took off running. What was that about?"

"Wow, what serendipity." She read admiration in the glance Pel threw her. "That day was weird," he said. "The previous afternoon, I had stopped to listen to the guy on the soapbox. When I left, he handed me a note. It was only two words, 'Meet noon,' and then someone grabbed the note. I guess the speaker made a mistake, but that made me curious and I came out the next noon to check. No one was on the soapbox, but the note grabber was there talking with an older man. He spotted me and ran. I chased after. Then I turned around to find the older man scanning my chip."

"You were IDed!" Hallie felt her eyes grow big. "What did you do?"

"Went back to the library feeling like a fool."

"Do you suppose that was connected with the Net going crazy and kicking you out?"

"There are no data to back that up." Pel leaned over the bridge rail. "Ran, I've got to catch a bus."

"Let's go then." Ran climbed up from the pond.

She really liked these guys. "Why don't we have a picnic next week? We can celebrate your questioning the NODE and everything."

Pel looked doubtful. "As soon as I pose this question I need to find my way home."

His face brightened. "But I've got transit tokens. Yes, picnic first. And with the credits from working this week, I can maybe afford a taxi home."

Too bad their mysteries didn't coincide. She intended to pursue her study of Kansas for Kansans, no matter what Liz said. But she wondered what that note passing and snatching had been all about. She hoped Pel would be all right.

Ran

an walked silently back to the Sloans' with Hallie. She and Pel had chatted like old friends.

As they approached the Sloans' block, Hallie said, "I like your friend. I've never known anyone to care so much about something that he'd . . ."

"Rocket off like that?"

"Mm, leave home. Every time I leave Mom, it's from our fighting, and I feel guilty and childish. He just goes and does it."

"Yeah, he has nerve," Ran agreed. He held the door for her.

She smiled at him. "Time for a makeup lecture." Her feet ran lightly up the stairs.

Ran's spirits rose. Even if those two did like each other, he didn't have to feel excluded.

Work, he had told Hallie with complete assurance, when she asked him what he did for fun, but was it really true? Something felt lacking. And that pile of scrap wood drew him. John was in the workroom. "Could I use some of your wood scraps?"

"Go ahead," said his boss. "What are you planning to make? You ought to be taking more time off from my backlog of work."

"I watched a boy sailing a boat in the park. Maybe a boat with sails to control remotely."

"Feel free to use the fab too. You could let it produce your boat."

Ran glanced at it. "Thanks. I want to construct it myself, but it'll be useful."

"Need other parts?"

"I think I can recalibrate a remote from your discards, if that's okay." A fun Sunday!

He searched the Sloans' bookshelves, ran a search on their Net and eventually found an eighteenth-century sailing trawler with single mast and sails on a sturdy frame.

Until encountering John's antiques, his mind had traveled in space. The boat was both child's play and challenging, delicate work. He felt like a kid for the first time in—forever? Not since he was a little kid helping old man Carver. He worked late into the night.

The next morning he whistled while repairing, scraping, glueing, and sanding a small walnut stand.

"You're sounding cheery," said John. Hallie made a similar observation at lunch.

To both he answered, "Yeah. I had no idea how much fun building a model boat would be. I want to finish it to sail at the park next weekend."

"For the picnic!" said Hallie with enthusiasm. She turned to her aunt. "We're going to the park when Pel comes back. Would you and Uncle want to come?"

Her uncle hmphed.

Betty smiled. "I'll help you prepare a basket of food. You three have fun."

Ran went back to work. He should be contacting Coach. He should be following that slim chance of tertiary next term. But he hadn't had any fun in a long time. And he'd never had friends before.

Next week then. After Pel left.

Pel

Pel logged on to the Net and breathed out his relief when the Net accepted his password. He called his parents anticipating their displeasure. "Next Sunday, I'll be home. Promise!"

Before he started making up lectures, he sent out his usual query for Mik's whereabouts. Leaning back, he considered his question for the NODE. He had to fit it all into one question. He wanted to know so much. Who had disappeared? Where had they gone or been taken? And always, always, why?

Start with the names he was most sure of: Sam Suzuki, Geraldine Ramirez, Father Dominic Rivera, Taylor Layton, Gabe Fletcher. Yes. A tiny ping alerted Pel to his screen.

"Amigo Pel? Is that you?" An answer! No face, but—allowing for a deeper postpubescent voice—the accent was the same.

"Mik? Is it really you? I've been trying to reach you for years."

"Sorry I never got to say good-bye. My parents got an emergency call and we were gone. Here we are on ship *Mirnyy Gorod* in the Kara Sea. Access to your hemisphere is intermittent. What luck that I am on when your query came through."

Luck! All this time Mik had been halfway around the world.

116

Eagerly Pel asked questions and Mik answered. Tales of storms, inconstant Net access, plans to follow his parents' path of exploring the best ways to grow food. "Nothing more important than feeding people." A flickering picture brought Mik's face to the screen briefly.

Pel grinned. "I see you're growing a garden on your face too."

"And your face so hairless!" Mik retorted. "Now that we are found to each other, we must stay in touch." Mik's image faded again, but they talked until the connection broke.

Mik found. Pel couldn't stop grinning. Nothing would stop him now. He'd go home, catch up on assignments. Share classes with Hallie—incentive to never miss a live one. No more Workless with its old men and zombies.

He'd found Mik! No more nightmares. New friends. The world was waiting—bigger than the village, bigger than Dodge. He went back to considering his question.

When the first curfew warning sounded, he realized one more thing he wanted to know. At the alley shortcut, he checked that no one was around, then whispered, "Typhus?"

A scrabbling noise and then a hand movement. "I didn't tell you my name. You must have met up with Fixer then."

"Yes, I did," Pel agreed. "Can you give me safe passage through the alley and tell me more about my being tailed?"

"Come through. Orders comes in from the bosses. We doesn't get told who or why. No order to harm, just follow. You escaped onto a truck. UncCharley couldn't watch you then."

"Animal Welfare picked me up. I was in danger of getting sprayed along with some coyotes. I'm curious. How do you live?"

"Our clan is diagnosers. I study the medical courses. UncLum be teaching me how to disappear with and without a cloak, the art of camouflage, he call it. Standing real still be the biggest trick—like a butterfly close its wings and look like a leaf—but it be hard."

Nearing the end of the alley, Pel didn't want to lose this fount of information. "Tell me about the clans."

"Aches clan is the best. We keeps our word. Not like Roman clan with their Julius and Tiberius. They wants power, see? Watch out if they gets sent out after you. They doesn't care how many bodies they leaves behind."

Pel shivered. "What other clans are there?"

Typhus hesitated. "Best I don't tell too much, but remember, Aches clan is loyal, see? I tried to help Fixer, but I hurt him instead. I am trying to make up for that."

They had arrived at the end of the alley. Disappointed, Pel said, "Thanks for your help." The boy disappeared, leaving him with more questions than before. How had Ty hurt Ran? And wasn't he too young to study medicine?

raming one question for the NODE was Pel's only haunt that night. His most successful research always began with the right question.

Monday morning at the EO the official checked him off and nodded his head at an inner door. "Recycle crew. Through there, up to the roof. Transport's waiting. Tell 'em you're the last."

Dressed in mask and gloves, Pel joined the sorting team. If that landfill was as old as they claimed, it should have long since decomposed, but the diggers kept coming in with more loads. What had once been hauled out of town was now excavated and returned for analysis and recycling. He wondered if the stench would ever leave him. Four dirty days of work, walking to the shuttle early, returning via an ancient, noisy transport back to Workless, thankful for time to wash off odors and grime before the eatery closed its doors.

Not what he wanted to do every day of his life, but the interruption gave him time to think without distractions of additional data while sorting glop from goo, metal, glass, and plastic. Behind their masks, the workers didn't talk much.

Once, a stack of newspapers came down the belt, still readable. Pel groaned as the printed words were unceremoniously sorted before they reached him. *Damnation, at the wrong station!* He wished he could have spotted a date and read a headline at least.

And always, the question for the NODE. Where were his disappeareds now? What about those strange words? Should he include them in the question? He thought not. That was too crazy, but . . .

But the words had stopped the Net cold. He had to include them.

Friday, he returned to his normal work crew in the indoor arena—litter detail—grateful to be smelling clean air while performing the humdrum task of scrubbing blood stains from a crash landing during a tournament game played the previous night.

He did need to include those strange words. And he'd add: ". . . what caused their disappearances and where are these people now?" Maybe. Maybe something like that.

Picnic

Pel

Saturday morning at the Plaza Coffee Bar, a regular stream of customers were ordering the special, most of them carrying their cups of Coffee-Mocha-to-Die-For onto the plaza, where they mingled with other business suits.

Inside, Pel sat across a little table from Mr. Esquivel y Turner's graying hair and young-old face. "Call me Turner," he'd said. The Infotech Department head wore standard business tan, a loose jacket and straight pants nubbly with a silken texture, a far cry from Jeb's rough-and-ready style.

Ran had vouched for Jeb; Jeb had vouched for his wife and boss, the city manager; she and Jeb had vouched for Turner. He guessed he'd better be completely open. Pel began his tale. Hoverbuses came and went several times before he finished. Throat dry, he sipped from his cooling cup of To-Die-For—hoping it wasn't.

The older man's eyes half closed in thought. "I can arrange a secure upload of your stored data. That's my business, after all, and part of your package when you purchase storage." Pel breathed a little easier. "Jeb told me a little of your inquiries," Turner continued, "but it's the computer reactions that truly fascinate me."

"Schizophrenic, do you think?"

"That would imply difficulties distinguishing between reality and fantasy. I don't believe the NODE has that particular curse, but possibly distinguishing between real and false, or between open and passworded data—those might give it pause."

Pel tipped his cup for its last drops. "Jeb said I might be able to pose a question directly?"

"Have you come up with one?"

Flicking on his tiny noter, Pel read it one more time before he passed it over:

How do these words, whistlestop, thyme-sage, crumbling pyramid, and rosemary, relate to the disappearance of the following people: Sam Suzuki, Geraldine Ramirez, Father Dominic Rivera, Taylor Layton, and Gabe Fletcher, and where are these people now?

He twitched. Something was missing still.

Turner read the display and nodded. "Why not? If you've invented this story of yours, you're one hell of a confabulator. Let's go to my office."

Pel followed Turner from the coffee bar. Three more words. He needed to add three more words to his question.

Ran

Ran heard the gate's call but kept to his adjustments. The remote wasn't as refined as he would've liked due to time constraints. He backed away and tested for distance.

"He's been like that all morning," he heard Hallie say.

"Hey, Pel," Ran said. The sail rose only partway. He went to adjust its rigging. With half an ear, he listened as Pel spoke to Corsair the cat, and rubbed its ears.

"The food's ready but Ran's not," Hallie said. "He wants to try out his boat when we get there. Tell me about village life while we wait."

Ran listened to Pel speaking of ecologists watching animals and plants slowly adapt to the land and the land to its users, of the cautious speech among village dwellers that overlaid an independence of thought. Then Pel asked Hallie, "You mentioned arcologies last weekend. Have you lived in one?"

"My parents bought a small apartment in the Tallgrass building before I was born, so yeah, I grew up in one. The gardens are lovely and I love taking care of the dog kennel."

Ran checked the boat's planks. "Almost dry," he said. "With those crosswalks, you never have to come down to the ground."

"He's paying attention?" Hallie gave a mock gasp.

"Must be ready to go then," said Pel.

Ran grinned up at them. "She's still a tiny bit tacky. I hope she'll dry as we go along. I think the sail's adjusted." He placed the remote in one pocket, tools in another, and picked up the boat.

Hallie collected the picnic basket. The cat followed, drawn to its appetizing odors. At the door she told Corsair, "Go see Aunt Bet.

122

We'll be back later."

The day was well advanced, the sun slanting from the west with a comfortable warmth. Hallie walked between the boys, carrying the basket of food until Pel took it from her, saying, "For what we are about to receive, I will labor gladly."

Friends, Ran thought. He had friends.

As they entered the gate, a woman carrying a toddler brushed past them. Her side-glance at Pel's gray coverall reminded Ran, now in street clothes, of similar looks he'd received. Small groups scattered through the shrubbery, many preparing to leave, collecting balls and belongings.

Hallie headed for a grassy area within sight of the pond. "Eat first." She pulled a cloth from the top of the basket and spread it out. Ran looked longingly toward the water, but his stomach grumbled. They demolished rolls filled with salad and rolls filled with a variety of salty, sweet, and nutty contents. When all was gone, they lay back, content to look at the sky.

"The Romans ate while lounging," Pel said. "Did they then sleep it off?"

"Or something," said Hallie with a snicker.

Ran picked up his model. "You'll know where to find me," he called over his shoulder. Pel waved a lazy hand. Hallie smiled, her arms folded behind her head, a peaceful look on her face.

Ran studied the pond, taking in the pair of tweens under the arched bridge skipping stones across the water, and the ducks vying for bread from a child on the far side. At the water's edge he launched his brave little boat, breathing in odors of moisture, plants, and something sweetly floral on the breeze. The brook trickled. The pond became calm seas, his sailing trawler bobbing on the wavelets.

The remote worked, after a fashion. Ran adjusted it. But oops, he'd misjudged the way the sails would respond to a real breeze. He kicked off his sandals and rolled up his pants to wade to the capsized craft, ocean god to the rescue. The ducks paddled farther away. Not exactly an ocean-going species. No matter. *Que importa?*

She needed a name, this little boat. Maybe *The Betty*. No, not quite right. She seemed to sing of ocean waves and breezes. Yes, she had to be *The Melody*.

A voice called to Ran, the ocean became a pond again, waters trickled softly.

Hallie stood above him on the bank. She repeated, "Pel's napping. I'm going to walk the perimeter trail."

He waved and went back to adjusting his control over the sails. Somehow, he was always a little off. *What's that? I thought you could fix anything?* said a cheerful voice in his head.

Even the wind? No way.

Hallie

The trail was soft, well trodden, and this late in the afternoon she had it to herself. Nearby houses were completely screened from view by shrubs and trees. Illusory isolation. She loved it, the birds, the thickets . .

Hallie's spirits bubbled. No food left—Aunt Bet would be so pleased. She'd had as much fun with Pel and Ran as she would have with Cass and Van. Over lunch they had talked about everything. She'd told them of the bombing, and of her theories why. Ran told of labor pirates and their methods. Strange how they'd all gotten a glimpse of something evil, and yet she felt so enthused by sharing their experiences.

And then, when the food was gone, Pel's astounding news. He was practically dancing with excitement. "Now if I can have the attention of both of you, I have an announcement. I found my friend Mik! He's the whole reason I got into this search for disappeareds, and turns out he disappeared only from my point of view. He's been living on some floating city in the Arctic Sea."

"The other side of the world," said Ran.

"Yes! Back to tertiary, here I come," Pel said, laughing. He flopped on the ground in a pose of total relaxation. "I've a lot of work to catch up on. I arranged a ride back for first thing in the morning."

Some sensation caused Hallie to look at Ran. "We've got to find a way to get you into a live tertiary program where you don't have to use virtual."

"Not that simple," said Ran. "Study materials also come in virtual."

"Exceptions!" she said. "You can get an exception."

Ran had shaken his head but looked slightly hopeful.

New friends! She smiled remembering Pel's sleeping face, slack but still appealing. She liked his dark, warm skin tones, his inquiring mind, so full of wide-ranging ideas. And Ran had risen in her estimation. They both had courage. Where she had declared her independence, Ran and Pel actually practiced it. She had to do better.

Compared to Pel, the other students felt distant and flat. Miguel might be smart and friendly, but she didn't think he'd be that adventurous. And now she'd get to see Pel during lectures and discussion.

The airy froth of her mood slowly dissipated, leaving her calmly cheerful. A good time to consider that essay on Mark Twain and the analysis of the great migrations, both due soon. She'd never known the park to be so quiet; even her footsteps made little noise.

Ran

Ran jerked upright. Ocean reverted to pond. He stepped into the muck to retrieve *The Melody*. The sun had dropped low. His ears flooded with noises, the gentle shushing of water flowing into the pond, a bird twittered.

Something had disturbed him. He wiped off the boat's hull thinking. The hum of an aircar, that was what he'd heard. Probably someone arriving at one of the nearby houses. But that particular hum had somehow invaded his peace. Parks were no-fly zones.

A scream.

Hallie! Ran flung himself through the shrubbery, ignoring the meandering path, ignoring his bare feet. Every step seemed to take an hour. He didn't know where he was going, except toward the cry. The park was too big. How far away was she?

A small silver Spark loomed ahead, parked, screened by bushes.

Ran arrived at its rear. No sign of humans.

No, there they were, two indistinct shapes coming from the other direction, dragging an inert body. Hallie.

He wanted to attack head on, but two against one? No, he needed to prevent their taking off. He ducked behind the sportscar, little knife already in his hand. Crouching, he felt for the seam of the car's access. His blade slipped easily beneath the flap since someone had already unsealed it to tamper with the aircar's prohibitions. He pulled

126

up the cover, but without a light, he couldn't see the car's brain.

"Set her down while I put this away," said one of them.

He had to stop the fuel, then. Ran sliced at the line and jerked back from the icy burn of decompressing gas. Every second an eternity. Too slow. The fuel had to dissipate.

Quick. Don't let them load Hallie. Keep them occupied. Keep them from lifting. Ran crept toward the front of the aircar.

Gold Hair backed into the car, struggling to pull Hallie's shoulders into the small compartment behind the seats. A dark-haired man held her feet.

Determined, lean, tough—these guys weren't playing. Ran knew himself no match for their years and training . . . But that was Hallie.

He pushed through screening branches to confront them.

Dark Hair hissed and dropped Hallie's feet as Ran hurtled forward. With a slight move, Dark Hair threw him down.

From far off Pel's voice yelled, "Stop!"

"Leave her. Let's go." Gold Hair shoved Hallie out and disappeared into the vehicle.

Ran half rose and threw himself at Dark Hair's legs, but managed to catch only one. Almost dancing, Dark Hair kicked Ran in the belly. A second blow landed on his temple.

Following Gold Hair, Dark Hair leaped into the Spark. "Lift now," he said.

Gasping, holding his belly, Ran struggled up. "No!" he shouted. "No! You can't lift." With the fuel still draining, the car would—

They lifted.

"NO!"

The sportscar rose one, two, six feet off the ground. It blinked out of sight.

He had failed. A few feet higher, the Spark reappeared, now

descending.

Ran flung himself at Hallie's prostrate body, toward her blue and green braid, her bright shirt. Blades of grass came nearer, slowly—*so s-l-o-w-l-y* . . .

The aircar fell with a deep thud.

A second later—*WH-O-O-O-M*!

Real Trouble

Pel

Security arrived along with the ambulance.

"Who are you? What happened? Do you know these people?" they asked Pel.

"I'm Peleus Teague. Three of us came for a picnic. Hallie Pollard and Ran Kenelm and I. After we ate, I fell asleep. When I woke, Ran was at the water, working with his boat. I got up to ask him where Hallie went. That's when we heard her scream. Ran started running. I was on the wrong side of the water. It took me longer to get there."

Pel shuddered. The park's layout had been his undoing. The pond had kept him from going straight after Ran. He had pounded over the bridge.

> *Panic, fury, foes, doom.*
> *Speed, fly, flit, zoom . . .*

He didn't know where Ran had gone. Down the most likely pathway, he paused to listen, impatient with delays.

What will be demanded?
Can I be ready soon?
No time to stumble, fumble, fall . . .

He'd sprawled over a protruding root. No time for songs in the head! Where were they? He scrambled up, pushed forward. Branches clawed at him, blocked his view. He broke free. Green park opened up. In the fading light, the aircar was a silvery blur.

"Then what happened?" demanded the Security officer.

Pel gulped and took a shuddering breath. "Two guys were carrying Hallie. Ran came out from behind the sportscar, a silver Harly Spark I think. Ran tackled the one holding her legs. I yelled and ran toward them. They dropped Hallie. The one who'd been holding her feet threw Ran down and kicked him. Ran got up and yelled for them not to lift, but they did. It rose, blinked out, then reappeared maybe ten feet up. Then it exploded"

Pel rubbed his face with the backs of his raw hands. Trying not to gag, he said, "Ran threw himself over Hallie's body. I rolled him over to put out the flames and dragged them both farther back."

Dissatisfied with his answers, one said, "Box him up."

A pox on their box! At Security headquarters, Pel sat enclosed behind an opaque shimmering curtain whose forcefield repelled him when he came near. His chair, made of strangely configured slats, dug into his back. He compromised by leaning forward, elbows digging into his thighs, resting his head on sore hands. The pain-relieving salve on his palms no longer worked. What did it matter? He was okay. Hallie and Ran were not.

He shivered. The curtain stirred the hairs on the crown of his head. Deaths, even accidental ones, meant big trouble. Pel is in jail. No bail? He's going to fail.

The curtain disappeared. Pel looked up. "Come with us."

Two officers—one male, one female—escorted him down a long hallway, Pel's footsteps tentative between them, to a small chamber where a man in a taupe suit introduced himself.

"Counsel Bilker, appointed by the court for your defense."

Bilker cleared his throat. "As these officers will have already informed you, you have the right to remain silent, but if you do not choose to speak, your silence may be used against you. If you do choose to speak, a brain scan is required, but that verifies only your belief in the truth of your statements. It is not proof of truth. Under the circumstances, as these officers have explained it to me, I do recommend that you be as open as possible so that they may proceed with their inquiries."

Pel nodded, said "I agree," and repeated his answers under the brain scan to the grim-faced officers. They seemed particularly interested in the aircar and its disappearing act. He sensed sympathy for his situation. A germ of hope took root that they might lay the blame where it belonged.

But all those burns. Pel swallowed. Ran might not survive.

Hallie

An unfamiliar beeping brought Hallie's eyes open. Mom sat beside the bed. White walls, white sheet. Her head throbbed. She reached up to feel, then raised both hands. Short, short hair.

Liz reached across their mother to take her hand.

"Liz. Why are you here? What? . . . Where am I?"

Someone blew a nose. Aunt Bet on her other side. Uncle Jack, his white, fly-away hair next to Aunt Bet's gray. They looked . . . endearing. Aunt Bet so much like Mom, her expression a mirror of Uncle Jack's.

"You're all right, love," said Liz. "You've been in an accident and we're all in shock. But you're all right."

"Accident? I haven't been anywhere. We were getting ready for the picnic."

Jeb came to stand at Liz's shoulder. "What's the last you remember?" he asked.

"Aunt Bet and I got the food ready. Ran kept working on his boat. Pel came. We were talking, waiting for Ran to finish—I think . . .

"Or did we start walking to the park?" Like sorting through a jumbled pile of memories, no sense to be made of any one piece. A glimpse of something, then something else took its place. She shook her head, stopping when the pounding intensified. "It's all mixed-up."

Jeb stepped back.

Hallie reached for her braid that wasn't there. "Am I going bald?"

"You're fine, dear." Mom looked as if she didn't believe her own words.

"I'm dying, aren't I?" Some horrible disease they hadn't found a cure for.

The nurse interrupted. "You are not dying, young lady. We've found traces of Doramnis in your blood. It causes amnesia. You've lost some hours out of your life."

"Did I do something?"

"No, love," said Liz. "Something was done to you."

"Pel? Ran?" The jagged jumble in her head moved into her chest.

"We don't yet know what happened," said Aunt Bet. "There was an explosion. You're all right. Ran's here in the hospital. Pel is—we don't know where."

"He's talking with Security," said Jeb.

"Explosion. Like that body bomb?" she asked. Someone must be dead.

"No bomb," said Jeb. "An aircar." Neither Pel nor Ran owned a car. The jagged stabbing inside softened a little. Not in the park then. Parks and streets were off-limits to aircars.

"What's wrong with Ran?"

"He was badly burned," answered Liz.

An explosion, they said. An aircar. What did it all mean?

The nurse announced that Security wanted to interview Hallie. Jeb and Uncle Jack went out and returned with a woman dressed in Security black who asked her what she remembered.

"It's Saturday. Pel arrived. The three of us were going to walk to the park for a picnic. What happened?"

"That's what we're trying to find out," the officer said. "Nurse, find out how long that substance lasts in the blood. How soon will she regain her memory? We'll need her testimony."

Horrible images peppered her mind. Doramnis. Body bombs. Did she attract violence or something? Everyone looked so grim. Her brow creased.

"You said Ran was burned. How did he get burned? What about Pel?"

No one would tell her.

Ran

Like a plant struggling to reach life-giving light, Ran moved slowly toward awareness. Tendril by tendril unfurled, bringing him upward by degrees. Increased awareness brought a thought. He was a machine guy. Why was he dreaming of plants?

Everything hurt.

Ran had never thought of pain as red, like looking through blood, but neither had he ever lain on a forge, blacksmiths pounding on the hot metal of his skin. Above him, voices argued.

". . . my patient . . ."

". . . question him . . ."

". . . still unconscious . . ."

"Indicator says otherwise." Gentle fingers opened one eyelid and a light played in and out. He started to follow the light.

A grim female voice said, "I will be right here. You ghouls have five minutes. He's not going anywhere for a long time."

The other voice, male, seemed to go on and on. "You were at the scene . . . a tool . . . your traces . . . caused the explosion . . ."

Explosion! A noiseless warning sounded in his head. His breath quickened.

He tried to shake his head but it wouldn't move. He wanted to explain, but couldn't seem to get his voice working.

The voice faded in and out. "We have your accomplices in custody. Two dead . . . explosion . . . murdered . . . no longer speak for themselves."

Accomplices? "Who . . . ?"

"You will tell us what happened. We're going to attach a brain scan to verify the truth of your words."

A testy voice broke in. "As your appointed representative, in absence of a court order, you have the right to refuse the brain scan. These men are being pressured to act."

"Ahm nah' lyin'," said Ran.

The woman's voice again. "Time's up. You'll have to come back. If called to testify to my patient's condition, I will say exactly what my instruments are measuring—that this young man is not yet fully cognizant and that you coerced him."

"We'll be back," said a voice with disgust.

"Dead . . . ?" Ran murmured. Not Hallie. Not Pel. He received no answer.

✴ ✴ ✴ ✴ ✴

How much time had passed, he had no way of knowing. He lay immersed in a tank filled with healing solution that kept his regenerating muscles moist. He'd lost more than skin, the medico told him. His back was blessedly numb. He wished his feet were numb too.

Figures hovered over him, but belly down, Ran saw only their black-clad Security legs and heard their rumbling voices.

A separate, higher-pitched voice was attached to gray-clad legs. "I'm Counsel Nagel. I am here to protect your interests, with your help. You have the right to refuse a brain scan. Anything you say may, and likely will, be used against you."

An officer broke in. "We have two deaths. We have grieving

parents demanding immediate judgment."

The other officer's voice held husky overtones. "Without a statement from you, we'll have to go after your accomplices."

He had no accomplices, only fellow victims.

"I'm not lying. A brain scan is okay with me," said Ran.

"Brain scan." A hand affixed soft contacts to his forehead.

"Tell us what you did."

"They had Hallie. They were kidnapping her."

"We don't want to hear about what you thought. What did you do? What were your actions?"

Breath hissed between Ran's teeth. No excuses. He listened to his voice narrate his actions.

"You admit there were three of you involved."

"No! I was the one who disabled the vehicle. The others had nothing to do with it—except they'd grabbed Hallie—"

"You're not in any shape to stand trial. Your confession will have to stand."

Counsel's voice cut in. "You have the right to a trial by jury."

"No," Ran said. They would drag everything out—his lack of a job, his place at the Sloans'. They would implicate Pel . . .

His body immobilized, Ran's memories thrashed and whirled. He groaned. Two dead. No way to bring them back. Two dead. *How dared they attack Hallie!* He'd done this to his friends.

Two dead. He'd be judged on the deaths, not the reasons why.

If only there'd been light to see by, he might have severed the aircar's brain instead of its fuel line. He'd known the danger of explosion. If only he'd run faster. If only he'd delayed them longer. Then they couldn't have lifted off and no damage would have been done. If only he could change the past. Two dead. Security, Justice, whoever—had blood in their eyes. He didn't want Hallie and Pel involved. He'd waived his right to a trial by jury.

Waiting

Hallie

Security ordered Hallie moved, saying she needed to be kept under observation. Her room was small, square, and windowless—the psych ward, she guessed, though no one said so. The room was pleasant enough. One wall was a virtual scene moving from forest to valley to plains so slowly that she was more aware of gusting clouds in bright blue skies than of the landscape's motion.

She triggered her journal. "What happened? Why won't they tell me? All they say is they don't want to create false memories. So they shut off my phone function. I feel like I'm in jail.

"I can't learn anything more about the boys. Ran's in the hospital for burns—from what explosion? Nothing makes sense. So I've lost my memory. How can telling me what happened create false ones—unless they're telling me something false? What did I do to be sprayed with Doramnis? No one tells me what's going on!"

She swallowed her desire to scream. Don't let them think she was going bonkers here! Staring at the panorama, she said, "I wish I were out there riding into that forest on horseback. Or even hiking into those trees with a backpack. I know it's silly, but I just wish I could be free of all this. Mom looks so concerned when she comes, and it's my fault—somehow. She doesn't say so, but it's got to be."

Her keepers allowed her lectures—in virtual. She kept thinking she'd catch up by week's end, but it didn't happen. Too many interruptions. Daily visits from the memory specialist, who acted like their sessions were cheerful chats between friends.

Right now she couldn't concentrate on a lecture. She got up to select a virtual exercise program. She wanted to get out of here, not give them reasons to keep her.

Ran

Ran lost all sense of time's passage in his small area surrounded by machines and the occasional human. He floated on his back in a vat; soothing, warm, almost pain-free.

That Spark at the park had to be the same direflier as the one on the day he had met Jeb. There must have been some purpose behind the attacks, but what? The fliers were dead and he was the one in trouble.

A chime announced the com, Counsel Nagel's face appeared on the screen overhead. He couldn't escape the man's insistent voice wanting him to wage a defense. Ran answered impatiently, "Death is death. Becoming a zombie is automatic, isn't it? Why bother with a trial? I've already told everything I know. It's on record. Why fight?"

The voice went on and on about a strong case, about his right to a jury of peers, about there no longer being a death penalty.

"Zombies are a living death. That's to be preferred? What peers?" Ran asked. "You mean they'd find me a jury of grounders? Why would they give me the time of day?"

That brought him silence for a space. "You're only fifteen," Nagel finally said. "You may have established your independence, but that alone does not make you an adult. I suggest you think it over." The man blinked out.

If only those two dead guys were facing trial instead!

Personnel came and went, some glancing at his instruments. One wearing the lavender of a hospital tech made an adjustment to one of them.

All was lost. He was headed for zombiehood—harmless, vulnerable, all violent impulses decommissioned. He didn't know if it was possible to reverse re-gening, but no one would bother to change an obedient worker ant back into something unpredictable.

When they made him a zombie, he'd lose his connection with machines. That was what he'd miss most. Face it—he loved machines. Their presence around his hospital space was comforting. Companionable. Their vibrations spoke to him in some strange way.

He listened to the vibrations . . .

Something had changed. The beeping monitor still read his vitals. The pump gurgled, circulating healing fluids over his damaged tissues. The medications shunt that fed in painkillers . . . That one—it wasn't working. His feet burned. He squirmed. Fire crept up his back, intensified—grew agonizing.

"Hey!" His voice sounded weak, as if he had nothing to push the words out with. He was breathing, wasn't he? *Use your breath. Use it!*

"Hey. Help!"

140

Pel

Pel had been interrogated several times in this same little room, always with the claustrophobic panic of fate closing in. His escort closed the door behind him. This time no one stood there physically to intimidate him, only a com screen. While waiting, Pel cataloged the scratches and stains on the scruffy table, the rough texture of gray walls.

Court-appointed Counsel Bilker's face appeared on-screen. "Arraignment is scheduled for next week. You will be tried as an accessory after the fact."

"So soon?" Pel asked.

"We have your spoken testimony. We have the statement of . . ." He referred to his notes, "of the saboteur, known as Ran Kenelm."

Bilker didn't remember Ran's name. *Probably doesn't even know mine.* Not fair.

"You were all present at the scene. Your leader takes credit for the explosion. We have only your word that an abduction was taking place."

"Abduction! What do you call the illegal presence of an aircar? One that no one noticed arriving. An aircar using a no-see-um."

The face on the screen was flat, unreal. "Understand, I'm presenting this to you from the prosecution's spin. The victims belong to wealthy, powerful families who will do everything they can to obscure any wrongdoing. They will portray the young men as sporting and having fun. The fliers are no longer able to speak for themselves. Evidence of any no-see-um was destroyed with the aircar. Do I have to repeat that one of you claims to be the cause of the explosion?"

"And what about Hallie? Can't she testify to the abduction? She was the victim, the one being snatched!"

"Unfortunately, or conveniently, the third member of your party claims amnesia."

"No memory? Why not?" demanded Pel.

"Her blood registered the presence of Doramnis, which is normally used on animals for capture and re-release without memory. She is unable to make a statement."

"Doramnis? That's the stuff Animal Welfare was complaining about being stolen."

"Yes. And there's another item counting against you. You have been identified as having been illicitly present in an Animal Welfare vehicle. Your proximity to Doramnis is a matter of official record."

"Your logic is all backward! Because I overheard that they had thefts, I'm supposed to have taken some? To use on a friend?"

"My hands are tied. Security's investigation has been completed. We have a statement by . . ." He checked his records, "Tobias Nordstrom of Animal Welfare."

"Who's he? What about the woman who picked me up?"

"Nordstrom's partner is on leave without pay, currently unavailable for comment."

"There's a perfectly reasonable explanation and she could back me up."

"Too late. Investigation's complete."

"I thought you were my counsel! What about appeal? What if I found eyewitnesses?"

"No appeal until completion of the present trial. You would again be assigned counsel by the court."

Good, Pel thought. Couldn't be worse than Bilker, could it?

"I will return in person to accompany you to court, in . . ." he looked away and then back, "in six days. Judge Crompton presiding. You will be notified of the time." Bilker's face blinked out.

Judge Crompton! Simpson, after throwing that rock, had seen Crompton the same day. And one day later a blank-eyed Simpson had returned to Workless. One of the men at Workless had said, "Judge Crompton doesn't allow for appeals. He makes sure of immediate action. That's why Security likes him."

The Zombie Judge. And he had to stand before Crompton in six days.

"Back to the conference room with you," said the guard.

Pel got off his cot. So soon?

In the dingy doorway, Pel blinked. Hallie's burly brother-in-law sat on the opposite side of the table. "Jeb. I thought you were going to be Counsel Bilker again. How's Hallie?"

Jeb waved him to sit and shook his head. "Confused, angry— otherwise well enough, thanks to you two."

Pel grimaced. "No, only thanks to Ran. I think I may have been the one to spook them into the air, since I came head-on from the other direction." He added in bitterness, "I should have gone with her instead of falling asleep."

Jeb interrupted. "Hindsight does no good. She also made her choices and none of you can alter what happened. She's rather distressed at losing her hair, but that will grow back. There she lay in the hospital, a hand to her head. 'Bald? Am I going bald?' she asked." Jeb's voice was a perfect mimicry.

Pel smiled briefly. Unfair. Even with no braid to cling to, she'd be appealing to him.

Jeb went on more grimly. "She has no memory, even of going to the park, but she does remember suggesting the outing. She's going to be even more distressed if the court rules—and the odds are that the judge *will* rule—in favor of those two *perversos*." Jeb spit that last word out. "One of them is a judge's son, the other from a media mogul's family. Judge Crompton is a friend of the one, afraid of the other, and refuses to recuse himself."

"Oomph." Bilker had suggested as much. "Do you know how Ran is doing?"

"Reports are that he's improving."

"Good!" A certain tautness eased. "But what's going on? I get a bit of Net headlines but nothing that tells me anything. My counsel won't look into counterarguments. I'm being framed by someone in Animal Welfare because I had been in one of their vehicles and it was their Doramnis that was used on Hallie. This is not a justice system at all. No one cares for the truth."

Jeb raised a hand. "If you keep your voice down, we can have privacy here." He gestured to a small cube on the table.

Pel leaned forward and lowered his voice. "My counsel, the incompetent, didn't ask me for any information beyond my statement to Security. I thought I had a challenge, finding the right question to ask the NODE. My counsel wouldn't know a question if he stuck his head in it.

"That Animal Welfare woman who picked me up—I think they put her on leave to keep from explaining that her partner didn't broadcast on implant level for the streets to clear. I didn't hear a warning. What if—what's his name—Tobias deliberately wanted me

144

in danger? I know. That sounds like a conspiracy theory—improbable, unprovable."

Jeb folded his arms on the table and hunched forward. "Conspiracy theory or no, the head of Animal Welfare, Buster Nordstrom, has affiliations with the People First organization. Someone might well be using him, and he might, in turn, be using his employees."

"Nordstrom? That was Tobias's last name too. What does this case have to do with the No Borders policy?"

"No bearing that we know of. But where there's one form of resistance, there are bound to be others."

Encouraged, Pel continued. "What if someone else witnessed what happened? What if others could add background, and coherence, to our story?"

Jeb pursed his lips. "Who . . . ?"

"I had a noid tell me I was being tailed. Maybe we were observed."

A bushy brow quirked up. "You certainly know how to hold my interest."

Pel related his experiences with Typhus. "If he could be found, he might tell us if anyone was watching at the park. Who knows what they might have seen?"

"A friend of the Fixer, eh? That lad has rare gifts." Pel thought he referred to Ran, rather than Typhus. Jeb slapped his hands on his thighs. "A task I'll enjoy undertaking. Typhus, eh? Maybe Betty would like to send a treat to him. But there's no way noids could come forward to testify."

"No." Pel drooped. What did the civilized world know about underdogs? That word again. He was haunted by dogs. And cats. Were there also undercats?

Jeb leaned his elbows on the table. "Okay. My turn to talk. I'm here to pass on the repercussions of your question."

Pel closed his mouth and swallowed. His question to the NODE.

"Picture this," Jeb continued. "Top government personnel madly juggling data like hot potatoes. Most data quashed before it could be made public, but—you can be certain—details will filter out slowly. Watch the news. I'm not in the know, but I'm told bits and pieces related to your question will be emerging daily.

"Meanwhile my boss is pulling strings. Don't expect fairness, but pay attention to everything that comes your way."

Pel returned to his cell, occasionally twitching into a grin. Turner pulling strings. *I knew he was a puppet turner! I'm not alone. No more groans and moans.* Or maybe Jeb meant his wife, the city manager. She could and would pull strings, too, for her own sister.

He grew more serious. Jeb's words—"Where there's one form of resistance, there are bound to be others"—The People First movement objected to free passage of people across borders; they were the same ones who objected to setting aside half the land for plant and animal habitats. They should be called the Me First movement.

But what did Jeb mean, watch the news?

Exile

Ran

The nurse didn't believe him that someone had switched off his medications, but not even the nurse could discover why the shunt had quit feeding. "Someone was here," Ran insisted.

"I'll check," said the nurse. But when he returned he reported, "Our scans show no one near this machine."

"Someone turned it off," Ran said again. A noid could've gotten by without being noted on the scanner, but a noid lived to be invisible, unnoticed, uncaptured. He didn't believe it was a noid. What if there was a way to block a chip's signal?

"Mr. Kenelm."

He recognized the voice. "Counsel Nagel. What brings you here in person?"

The tank holding Ran revolved. Now he could see the man frowning down at him.

"I have bad news. Most extraordinary proceedings I've ever seen."
Ran took a deep breath.

Counsel Nagel cleared his throat. "Your arraignment was
scheduled for next week. I need not tell you that I would have filed
for immediate review had you been sentenced to be re-gened. Your
records do not warrant such treatment, and your employers, the
Sloans, speak highly of you. But this . . . This is the first time I've ever
been given a writ of supersedeas. The NODE orders you forthwith to
leave Earth. Without trial."

The man's words made no sense at all. Leave Earth?

"Without any hint of the reason, you are to immediately embark
on Interstellar Ship *Orpheus*. You leave in two days. Your medico is
most unhappy with this unusual state of affairs, as am I, though for
quite different reasons, I assure you."

Shipped out. Not become a zombie. Ran laughed weakly, until
his throat tightened and his nose tickled. "What did you say?"

"Exile is not an established penalty. Our system does not call for
exile for any crime. And without a trial, you have not been sentenced.
No dates of return are mentioned. I shall immediately protest the lack
of legal precedence, but I'm afraid the directives for your departure
must stand. That is the nature of writs of supersedeas."

Medico Gupti bustled in, speaking to someone not present. "You
can't sleep him. His skin cells are spreading nicely, but until deep
healing has completed, I forbid sleep. Patient's chart please."

A note sounded. His tank rotated again. Medico Gupti ignored
his counsel's presence as she embarked on a technical discussion with
what must be the ship's medico. Ran withdrew behind a shadowy wall
of disbelief. Sleep meant a long voyage, not local asteroid mining.

"Where am I going?" he asked his counsel's dark gray legs.

Someplace uninhabitable. Someplace full of rejects. Someplace with no choices, no options, no return. He swallowed. Look on the bright side. He wasn't becoming a zombie. He was leaving the planet.

"That information appears to be classified."

Addressing the floor, Ran added, "And my friends? What of them?"

"I do not yet have that information. I need not repeat that we will do everything possible to appeal this writ. However, the writ has tied our hands with this immediate departure date."

Ran took a deep breath. He'd done everything he could to protect Pel and Hallie from his actions. It would have to be enough. He was about to leave everything behind.

Hallie

At first she'd missed her family. She'd asked why they couldn't come more than twice a week. But now Hallie's small room felt crowded. With not enough chairs, everyone stood, emitting a nervous energy that left her uneasy, like she was watching an ill-prepared dress rehearsal. Except, this was real life. But then, her drama coach always said, "Real life is nothing but one dress rehearsal after another."

Just think of it as a play, she told herself. The cast:

Her mother playing herself—but really, really upset about something.

Liz—with that calm, set face she used on newscasts when she had to announce bad news.

Jeb—absolutely poker-faced, but radiating anger. He'd often

infuriated her with his teasing, but she'd never seen him like this. He stood behind Liz like a . . . like a rock wall.

Aunt Bet and Uncle Jack—looking concerned, worried, helpless. Hallie's stomach began to hurt. All because of an aircar explosion?

A knock. Celeste White—a former classmate of Liz's who had been the family lawyer as long as Hallie could remember—entered and said a few words to Liz, before turning to Hallie.

"Have you come to get me out of here?" Hallie asked.

"Hallie, I have some upsetting news for you."

Ran was dead. Or was it something about Pel? She took a breath and reached for the braid that wasn't there. "What's going on?"

"We've had an order from the NODE," said Celeste. "I've explored options and there are none."

"What order?" Her imagination boggled. The NODE? Why would a stupid network computer care what she did?

"Orders to send you three off-world," said Liz with crisp, cut-off words. Just like one of her newscasts. "You and Pel and Ran."

The room whirled. Hallie grabbed a chair back. "Off-world? Like exiles? How can they? It's crazy!"

"Unfortunately," said the lawyer, "the NODE seized upon the fact that you registered your independence as an adult and it is treating you as such."

Her mother gave her an accusing look.

"I did it so . . ." No point in explaining her stupid reasons.

Liz's face was still set, though she'd lost some of her calm. Was Jeb angry for her, or for Liz, or about something else? Hallie could feel all their emotions and none of her own. All just a dream. Surreal, like those floating clouds in the panorama.

"I don't believe any of this. How can anyone send me—us—away?

Pel and Ran didn't apply for independence. Did they?"

The look in her mother's eyes was like when her father died.

"I'm not dead! This is crazy! What do you mean off-world? Nobody's colonized any worlds yet, and I don't want to go anyway, so how can they send me? No world has passed all the studies and gotten all the permits. Or do you mean like to Mars? Why should I go anywhere?"

She fixed her eyes on her sister, always there to rescue her. "Liz! Liz, this can't be! It's impossible. Since when do—"

"Hallie, love, this is out of my power to change. It's out of Celeste's power. And if I could, I'm not sure I would."

"What . . . do you mean?" She felt cold all over. Her own sister was sending her away.

Liz gripped her hand, tight. "Remember that bombing? And what you discovered? Think about it. Do you want your life to be used against me? Don't get me wrong. I'm terrified for you. But if this will prevent something worse . . ."

What could be worse? Nothing could be worse.

Celeste, on Hallie's other side, vibrated with nervous anxiety. How did a lawyer measure success when she'd already said she could do nothing. Celeste kept her voice slow and soothing. "There's no way we can stop this from happening."

Hallie stared past them. On the panoramic wall, a bobcat stalked something unseen. "Tell me what is real about all this."

She swung back to the real people, away from wind that she couldn't feel, from pine boughs she couldn't touch.

"I'm in tertiary. I just want to finish my classes. You tell me someone gave me amnesia. And now the NODE says I have to go away. Is it because I'm a second child?" She hated saying it, knowing her mother would take the blame on herself. But she had to ask.

Celeste shook her head once, then stopped as if unsure.

It was Jeb who answered. "The three of you are in a bad position. The courts are after you because of the unexplained deaths of two *malos* who belong to powerful families. The NODE has not explained itself. Neither Ran nor Pel has any standing, and you've been linked with them. It appears that the NODE is taking on powers it hasn't been given and none of us has the power to stop that order. And yet, there is something protective about removing you three from the conflict."

"I'm not leaving," Hallie said. "Wait, how can Legal Net tell me my application is just a 'legal fiction,' and then use it against me?"

A tap on the door. "Time's up," someone outside announced.

Jeb and Celeste went out first. Her sister gave her a hug that left her breathless. Her mother's hug was gentler but more smothering, one hand pressing the back of Hallie's head. This was not happening. She needed to get out. Breathe some air.

Hallie followed them. A uniformed arm stopped her. Two guards stood on either side of the door. It slid shut. She pushed on it. Locked in.

She turned back to the panorama, a flat window with a 3-D scene. In the far distance, a line of horses and riders moved away behind trees. In the foreground, the bobcat bounded after a rabbit. She slammed her fists into the picture wall. The scene shivered.

"I want to go home!" *Thud.*

"This can't be happening!" *Slam.* Shivering grasses. Shivering bobcat.

"I'm not crazy!" *Thump!* She hammered at the smooth, peaceful scene. Again. Again.

Wilderness disappeared. Hallie met the eyes of a startled nurse where trees had been before. Her only other visitor each day.

"You've been watching me! Spying! I'm not crazy! I'm not sick!" Or was she? Her loss of hair. Locked in. If not sick, what was she? "Why are you doing this?"

A hiss of gas preceded an astringent medicinal scent. Hallie's fists unclenched. She sat on her bed. For a moment, the universe seemed to make complete sense. It was all right.

She yawned. Snuggled down on her pillow. Everything would work out.

Somehow.

Pel

Headlines scrawled across Pel's screen. Same old airball tournament.

Phoenix Team Goes Up in Flames; No Hope of Rebirth This Year

Dragons Put Meteors Down

His Workless assignment cleaning up bloodstains after games had been enough of a thrill.

New Breathable Planet Discovered

Pel straightened. Now that was an interesting item. Earthlike planets were still rare and important.

Slavery Charges Filed against AstroMining Co.

AstroMining. Slavery?

His door clicked open. "Come along. Bring your belongings."

Pel grabbed his pack, returned to him from Workless, and followed his escort to the desk, where a Security clerk IDed him, then read aloud from his screen: "Pending final resolution of your case, you are being released without prejudice into the care of Mr. Esquivel y Turner."

"What?" Maybe Turner had come to deliver the NODE's answer to his question. But Jeb had already. . .

No, he'd spoken only of the reactions to his question. Pel had yet to receive an answer.

The clerk looked up. "Do you object? Do you know the man?"

A sense of caution caused Pel to ask, "What are my alternatives?"

The clerk shrugged and looked at his records. "We have no reason to keep you here any longer. Your only alternative, since you're less than full legal status, is to be remanded into the charge of your parents until your case is heard."

Home. Longing filled Pel, deep-rooted, painful longing for home. But he couldn't take this trouble home. "No. I'll go with Mr. Esquivel y Turner." The man with the code to the NODE.

As if on cue, Turner emerged from the hallway with the elevator symbol, and greeted Pel, but said nothing more during their fast-paced walk back down the same hallway and their ascent to the rooftop. In the waiting aircar, Turner ordered, "Proceed on course."

They joined a traffic lane above Dodge, heading west.

Impatient with Turner's silence, and uneasy, Pel asked, "Where are we going?"

Turner tilted his seat to study him. "Understand, you don't really have a choice. But if you could choose, would you follow where your mystery leads?"

"What's going on? How do you have the authority to remove me from custody?"

"I asked first."

Turner pulling his strings again. "You ask would I continue following the mystery, but you say I have no choice. What difference does it make?"

Turner remained silent.

As soon as Pel had found Mik he'd been ready to ditch the rest. But was he, really? He still had a mystery to solve. With a sigh, he said, "I left home to find answers."

"Fair enough." Turner pulled a flat device from an inner pocket and handed it to Pel. Its gold case fit comfortably in his palm. "A databank. Jeb thought you might be interested in his interview with your noid. Simply tell it 'affidavit.'"

Pel said, "Affidavit."

The databank triggered a square holovid. Pel thought at first that he was looking at a rather dirty blank wall. Then Typhus's figure flickered in and out of view.

"For truth, then, I'll tell you what I saw."

Typhus had been there! He'd had no idea.

"So they sprays her with something. She scream loud when she first see them, but she go down fast with the spray. They drags her to their car. Fixer ran to the back while they arrives with her at the front and he do something quick-like. They hauls her almost inside. Then the Fixer's friend yell. You should have seen them jump. They drops the girl and says, 'Let's go.' Fixer, he run forward. He shout 'NO.' They

155

lifts. Their no-see-em blink on when they gets up higher than the bushes. Then it blink off.

"And Fixer threw himself on top of the girl." Ty made a choking sound. "They sit in the air for a sec, then they drops. There be a loud crash. Then it explode."

The holovid faded. They had a witness! But noids had no legal voice.

"Where are we going?" They must be over his village by now. He spotted the distinct demarcation between the greenhouses and cultivated lands of humans and the sea of gray-green prairie. On the horizon, the Rocky Mountains couldn't be distinguished from hazy clouds. Still miles ahead, the new capital bulged into the area set aside for the wild. There had been lots of negotiating for that land.

"Where are we going?" Pel asked for the third time.

Turner looked at him. "That databank contains your accumulated data store. Also included is the NODE's response to your question— on a time lock. By the time you get where you're going, you should be able to access some answers. As might have been expected, your question opened up a Pandora's box of revelations."

"How long a time-lock?" Pel wrestled with panic, thoughts whirling. "By the time I get where?" His voice shook.

"Your immediate destination is Denver Shuttleport. You have a writ of supersedeas. Your parents have received a copy. There's a copy in your databank."

"The shuttleport? Are we meeting a ship?"

"No, you are embarking on one. Take a look at your writ of supersedeas."

How could Turner sound so calm?

The voice of every villager who told Pel to leave well enough alone yammered in his skull. He was about to be disappeared! Never once had he considered space as the dumping ground for the missing. He swallowed hard before saying to the databank, "Writ of supersedeas."

Words streamed past as the device read aloud: "IN ACCORDANCE WITH DIRECTIVE 912-3200-5963, FROM THE DEPARTMENT OF JUSTICE, PELEUS TEAGUE, ID . . . IS REMANDED TO INTERSTELLAR SHIP ORPHEUS. ALL OTHER CLAIMS ON HIM ARE HEREBY SUPERSEDED."

Interstellar! No wonder he couldn't find the people he'd been searching for.

Turner said, "Blame it on the NODE, if you will. I've never before known it to be wrong. In this case, we have no idea what tortuous path of logic the NODE is following. And there's worse to come. Your friend Haldis Pollard, the victim of that attack, has also been ordered off-world. You are going to have to be the one to . . . to hold her hand, so to speak."

"Hallie!" His burst of gladness evaporated in a flash of shock. "Hallie? Even the NODE's logic can't be that convoluted. There's something else going on."

"You're a reasonable person," said Turner.

No he wasn't. That nightmare wave of cyclopean proportions again roared down, he couldn't breathe . . . hear . . . think . . . drowning in horror. Hallie. He'd dragged Hallie into his worst nightmare—and no doubt hers. And even her family couldn't stop it? His stomach tightened.

"Hallie and I are going wherever my missing people went? Are they even alive? That headline 'Slavery Charges against AstroMining'— are we to be slaves too?"

"Use your head." Turner remained calm. "If there are slavery charges, Justice is already involved."

"And Ran?"

"He, too, is shipping out." Turner pointed at the aircar com. "Call your parents now before we reach the port. They need to hear from you. My com's secure."

"Why are you involved at all? Why not Security? If this is an official writ, why aren't officials delivering it to me?" He clenched his shaking hands into fists. "What if I had chosen to be returned to my parents instead of into your custody?"

"The writ overrides everything else. Instead of me, Security would have delivered you to the spaceport—and you'd have no chance to call your family. I told you I'd track you down with the NODE's answer. You have your databank.

"You're endowed with great curiosity," Turner continued. "You've shown yourself strong enough to break loose from expectations in order to follow clues on your own. I think you'll bear up under this next challenge, after your initial shock."

Pel didn't feel like justifying Turner's expectations. "Why does Hallie—the ultimate victim—have to be drawn into this?"

"You don't have much time. Call your parents now."

Pel hadn't spoken with them since the day after the explosion. Recognizing reasonableness, he directed the com with a shaking voice. Facing his mother was even worse than he'd imagined. Following that difficult conversation, Pel interrupted his father's plans to combat the unfairness. "You need to know, I have to go."

He paused, memorizing their faces. "I love you. Don't give up on me. I'll be back. After my last promise, my word may not be worth much, but somehow, I will get back. And my disappeareds too."

"More adventure than you bargained for?" asked his father.

"For sure," Pel said. He couldn't bear to look at his mother.

His father, face creased with impotent grief, had the last word. "Be careful then."

His parents faded with the connection. They'd be waiting for what would seem like an eternity. He felt sick, betrayed. Hallie must feel even worse. Try crucified! Dead alive.

> *Pel rhymes with swell, as in swelled head.*
> *He dared to dwell in the city instead,*
> *Let curiosity rule while feeding himself on Workless's gruel—*
> *which rhymes with fool—and mystery's tool—and stubborn mule.*

PART THREE

ORPHEUS

Spider strode across the arcology rooftop and got into his aircar. His two Peacers dead. Incompetent tools! "Secure setting," he ordered and woke his tooth phone. "Tech." He wanted answers.

"Sir."

"How do you explain what happened?"

"I've been warning you. The Brain's beginning to think for itself. My hands are tied."

The Brain thinking to the extent of removing those kids from his sphere? If what Tech said was accurate, his web was about to unravel.

"Keep me posted on this thinking Brain of yours." Spider ended the call.

Every tool had its limits, and every tool also had a weakness to be exploited. Tech cared only about his Brain. Fortunately, Spider had other tools. An accident to the ship could and would be arranged.

He made a second call. "Put my ship on alert. I'm coming in to give orders."

It was time to end that mining operation for good. Collect his loot and wipe the evidence. But that Brain knew far too much. Many more revelations and he'd have to evacuate from Earth.

That was not going to happen.

Spaceport

Ran

Ran came out of the healing tank as wobbly as a newborn. Not only wobbly. Helpless. Dependent. He reclined on a wheeled seat, still shaking from the ordeal of being dressed in what the med tech called a gel pack--a thick, rubbery suit with a turtle-like bulge to better protect his back, leaving only face and hands exposed.

"Feel like I'm going deep-sea diving."

"You're doing well," the tech answered. "Tissue regrowth takes time, and it'll be slower in space. You'll live in this gel pack on the ship until your skin is back. The current infusion should last until you meet with your ship's medico."

Ran tested the painkillers in his system by working his arms. How had his hands escaped burns when the rest of his backside hadn't. He must have wrapped them around Hallie. *He flung himself—time slowed—over her prone body.* He bit his lip—hard. *Stop!*

The med tech swung around again. "I almost forgot. You've got a couple of messages." She handed him two tiny discs. Her cheerfulness emanated from another planet altogether. Messages? Must be from people yelling at him.

He yelled, "No! You can't lift!" The hatch slammed shut. The silver Spark rose. It blipped out of sight. Then blipped back into visibility. He flung himself . . .

"You're going to break them," warned the med tech.

Ran dropped the discs into the bag on his lap.

Two uniformed guards escorted him to the ambulance that would take him to the shuttleport. The hour-long flight became a new ordeal: no more quiet hospital, thick suit pressing on his raw, skinless back. Not pain, but fear of pain. Fear of going up in flames all over again.

At the shuttleport, they paused for a long moment during his scan.

"ID VERIFIED." Then: "BY PRIME DIRECTIVE, ADDITIONAL DATA ARE NOW STORED ON RADIO FREQUENCY IDENTIFICATION."

Radio frequency. It hadn't been a noid turning off his pain meds. Someone had found a way to block the chip's emanations. *Additional data.* Maybe the new data on his chip finally identified his parents. Sludge! No way to find out.

On the shuttle, his guards wheeled him into a small room labeled Special Needs Compartment, strapped his wheels to a restraint, and left. Being in the gel pack was like living in a clammy puddle. He'd always wanted to experience being surrounded by all the technology of a spaceship, but not this way. He missed the peaceful hospital, the warm fluids, the machinery. Eyes closed, he managed to identify only the fan circulating air.

Garbled announcements woke him from a doze.

After a long, long groggy wait came the rumble of engines. The pressure of liftoff threatened to sear his back nerves. They said you forget pain. He didn't believe it. The gel pack might not last until Space Dock. Panting, he kept his eyes on the screen as jets pushed them away from Earth's gravity. Acceleration remained constant.

At last, weightlessness took over. Ran took a deeper breath. Space Dock spun slowly, gleaming above the curve of Earth, but what caught his attention was an enormous gray-black dome, partially eclipsed by Space Dock. Dull thumps announced their arrival.

"Okay, way is clear for you now," announced a deep voice behind him.

"What is that?" Ran pointed at the huge object.

"Interstellar Ship *Orpheus*."

"Never heard of it. What I wouldn't give to tour *that* baby! Is it new?"

"Several years old but state of the art." Still unseen, the attendant released his tether. "We're going to attach you to the rail and whisk you through to your berth."

Wheeled like a baby, Ran zipped through one tube after another, then through an airlock, to come to a stop in a tiny compartment.

"You're not on board yet and your equipment isn't hooked up so don't try to use it. It's easier to get everyone settled in modules and then loaded."

"Just like cargo," Ran muttered.

"That's it," agreed the deep voice. "Ship utilities, food and drink stations to your right, toilet behind that panel ahead of you. Weightless rules apply. You familiar with them?"

"Yeah," Ran growled. He'd studied all he could about space.

His conveyance was secured with a click. "Here's your patient," his attendant announced. Unable to turn, Ran listened to the shuffle of two people swapping places behind him.

"I'm the ship's medico. My name's Eric Renal."

Ran saw first the uniform of turquoise with space-navy trim, then met dark brown eyes in a round, cheerful face. "You're the one who spoke with Medico Gupti at the hospital."

"In some pain, eh?" Medico Renal directed a scan over his body. "You'll feel better as soon as we get you settled—but I'm afraid you won't enjoy liftoff. We'll put you on your belly for now. Still a few hours before departure. Lean forward."

Ran landed face down on a padded ledge. The medico leaned over to meet his eyes.

"You'll be okay for a while. Nothing like weightlessness for that. You're strapped so you won't fly off. Meanwhile, I've got a dozen youngsters to ready for sleep. You may as well rest if you can." He added, "I'm afraid you'll feel the acceleration."

"So what else is new?" Ran asked, his voice thick. *A dozen youngsters?* Who?

Hallie

Behind the panorama, Hallie knew her keepers were watching, but she ignored them to focus on the slow movement of clouds in the sky. Anything was better than thinking about that meeting two days before. They could stop her feelings, but they couldn't stop her memories—aside from those missing hours, of course.

A click signaled an incoming call. "Hallie?"

"Mom!" Hallie's hand went to her ear. "Mom, I thought they turned off my phone."

Her mother took a shaky breath. "They did, but . . . they're allowing me one last call before you're . . . transported."

Transported. Exiled. Wiped off the face of the Earth. She could think of terms, she just couldn't feel anything. And yet . . . "What did I do?"

"Nothing, dear. You did nothing at all to cause this. It's . . . You got caught up in something, Liz says."

But she'd disobeyed Liz. "Then it was my fault." The stab of regret surprised her. She was used to the inhaled drug SereneAll tamping down all feeling. She cut off her mother's "No!" with a choked, "I'm sorry, Mom. I'm sorry."

With a soft hiss, her hidden keepers pumped more SereneAll into the air. Hallie made a face at them.

"Security says I can't see you to say good-bye, so they allowed this one call."

"Mom, I love you." She'd been such a bad daughter. All those fights.

"I love you too. My baby. Stay well. You'll be back. Liz promised." An empty silence replaced Mom's voice

"Liz," Hallie attempted. No connection. The panorama displayed a scene of the Rocky Mountains with rolling plains in the foreground. Denver lay in that direction. And the shuttleport.

She must have done something, but Hallie found she didn't care. Before she lost all feeling, she sent a thought to turn on her journal function, an adjunct to her tooth phone, a gift from her father before his death. "Daddy. I wish you were still here with us. Watch over Mom, will you?"

The SereneAll took effect. Somehow, somewhere, everything made sense.

A tap brought Hallie upright. "Time to go," said her memory specialist.

Hallie got off the bed and walked steadily to the door. She was being called upon to join the universe.

Pel

Immediately after Esquivel y Turner's aircar landed at the spaceport, uniformed officials escorted Pel onto the shuttle.

Stomach churning, anger burning—he should've gone home when he had the chance. But he'd had no chance, almost like the Fates—or Furies—had taken charge of his life. How had he managed to do all this—betray his friends, fail his parents, get exiled—in the space of three weeks, almost four? He should never have left the village.

His chest burned. He could never make up for the pain he'd caused Mom. And Hallie! He could come up with no reason for the NODE to justify the exile of a victim.

The passenger compartment was mostly empty seats facing a dark viewscreen. No Hallie. The few already seated were young. And subdued. Pel plumped down in the front row and held up his arms for the seat to web his torso. An acid cold invaded his gut. All his fault, asking that question of the NODE.

Official voices came over the intercom periodically, giving instructions. Pel only half listened. He'd been the perfect puppet, bobbing up and down on Turner's strings—taking Hallie and Ran with him. He stared down at palms no longer sore. Bright pink contrasted with his normal dark caramel. Got off lightly, hadn't he?

A girl slipped into the seat next to him. Chin-length black hair swung forward blocking his view of her face as she bent down to tuck a bag between her feet. She sat back, allowing her seat's webbing to tighten around her. At her sideways glance, he caught a flash of blue, even as he noticed the shape of her eyelids. Her genes were as mixed up as his own.

"Where are you heading?" he asked.

She shook her head. "I don't know. Wherever my parents are."

"Parents?"

"Aren't you? I thought this flight was chartered to get us to the ship."

"Mine are on Earth." Pel tamped down memory of distraught parents.

Her eyebrows drew together, head tilted. "A week ago, Children, Youth and Family officials came to my foster family and said I was to be returned to my parents. Order of the NODE. Asap. Shuttle and ship chartered for that purpose."

"Yes!" He smacked fist into palm. Those three words he'd added to his question: *and their offspring*. Turner had spoken true. He *was* going to get answers after all. The real deal.

At the girl's widened eyes, he grinned. "I've been working on a mystery, a puzzle of missing persons. One clue was the number of unexplained fosterlings during certain years. You must be one of them." He looked around. "You said chartered. Then this shuttle is for the fostered kids? My name's Pel. Pel Teague."

"Aryn Suzuki."

"Suzuki? Sam Suzuki is your father?"

"I don't know." She frowned. "All my life I've wondered about my parents. I used to draw faces, using my own features, trying to guess. Just now, they added extra data to my chip. I keep wondering what."

Pel shivered. "I have a databank with a time lock. Some governmental authority is being way too sneaky—or else they're delaying publicity. Maybe both." *Trapped. How apt.*

The shuttle began to lift.

"You weren't any too early. Did we almost leave without you?" Pel asked.

"Not me. Another girl was upset. I stopped to help, but they sent me on. I think they drugged her."

Uh-oh. "Light-brown hair?"

"Yes. Very short hair."

"Hallie." His webbing stopped him from looking back.

She shouldn't be here! What was the NODE thinking? No computer really thought, that was the problem. It churned out evaluations to be taken as law. But not Hallie! Why? Why? Why? He pounded fists on knees, until he caught Aryn's concerned glance.

With a sigh, he said, "It's a long story and I'm not sure why the two of us are here, especially why *she's* here. She's going to have a bad time."

Acceleration pushed them back into their seats. On the screen, Earth revolved and dwindled. Curiosity drew his attention back to his silent seat partner. "Aryn, you, um . . . how do *you* feel about being yanked away from everything?"

She pulled her eyes from the screen. "It's hard, isn't it? I loved my life and my foster family. But I knew something was about to happen."

"You knew?"

"There's a feeling." She seemed to search for words and then shook her head. "It's like being bored. It's like something saying 'Pay attention because this won't last.' If you do everything that needs doing, then when the call comes, at least you're ready." She made a grimace and gave a little shake of her head. "That doesn't mean easy. I hated saying good-bye to Ammi and Abbu. But all my life I've been wondering about my parents. You can't say *not now* when the time comes."

"Wow!" Pel said. "You find an order to the universe then."

"Chi," she said. "Synergy. Inexplicable things."

"And synchronicity, since you brought me news of Hallie."

"You say she's not a fosterling?"

"No. She and I are caught up in something else."

Aryn's eyes narrowed. "Then she doesn't have anything to look forward to?"

"We—my theory is . . . No, I'll just tell you our story." And for the next hour he spoke of the disappearances that caused him to leave his village for Dodge City in search of answers, of meeting Ran and Hallie, of the opportunity to ask the NODE his question, of the picnic that ended in a kidnapping.

"Ran disabled their aircar, but he couldn't stop them from lifting. It exploded in midair. Ran was severely burned. Hallie was sprayed with Doramnis by the kidnappers and consequently has no memory of it. But I can't understand why the victim would be thrown in with . . ."

Hallie. The love of his sixteen years.

He directed his mind back to the mystery. "Actually, I think Ran's the keystone. He's a fosterling too. Somehow, my question and that kidnapping pulled us in after him."

Into what he didn't know.

Stomach burning, mind a-yearning, time would provide answers.

Or not.

Space Dock

Ran

Ran woke to the sound of thuds. Still belly down, his harness jerked as his room swung to fit into place on the ship. Modular shipping. Cargo loaded and unloaded by container, passengers too.

"Welcome to Orpheus." Medico Renal floated back in. "All compartments are hooked up now. We're waiting on a systems check before we take off. Once on our way, you'll spend increasing amounts of time exercising in virtual."

Ran's eyes opened wide. He craned his neck to look at Renal. "I don't do VR," he said in a flat voice. "It doesn't work for me."

"Why doesn't virtual work for you?"

"Don't know. When I put those contacts on, I shut everything down. Like my brain shorts out the system."

"We'll be in space for a long stretch. Easier to sleep people than to keep their bones strong and muscles fit. Leaves more room for crew. You are my one exception. You have to do as we do—'vexing' the crew calls it. I don't know if you *can* fool all your muscles, and especially your bones, without virtual exercise, but while your skin is healing, it's your only option."

"Acceleration ought to be sufficient for my bones," said Ran sourly.

"Not!" replied the medico. "The drive provides a light constant gravity, but that's not enough. Vexing can work every muscle and somehow manages to fool the bones. With your current lack of skin, vexing is our *only* way to shape you up. Medico Gupti absolutely insisted that you not sleep—and you want to throw away your body, your future?"

He was a throwaway. Ran repeated, "I short it out every time."

"You can't short it out without a cause. It's up to you, you know."

"It's always been up to me."

"You sound bitter."

"I've only ever been able to trust machines—and now look! Pitted against the one machine I could never work with."

"Then it's meant to be. Nothing happens by accident." The medico straightened; his trajectory sent him toward the door, making weightlessness look easy. "Only life support is working until hook-up systems have checked out. Try to sleep." Renal floated out.

The door slid closed.

What did he mean, it's meant to be? Ran shut his eyes. The past had come back to haunt him. And now the medico . . .

But he was right. Low ship grav . . . When they arrived—wherever that was—he needed to be strong. Ran stared at the floor. VR to fool the brain that his body was exercising? If he could manage vexing, he might even consider tertiary.

Who was he trying to fool? Tertiary levels were on Earth. He hadn't applied.

But he had to show the medico—and not take the ship's brain down with him.

Aloud, he said, "I'll try. Once."

He shut his eyes. "Later."

Pel

In the relative weightlessness of Space Dock, Pel's stomach felt light, like racing downhill on his bike. The seat webbing released one passenger at a time. Those behind him had already disappeared through the tube. Someone retched, causing Pel to swallow hard and focus on his every movement. He lost sight of Aryn while learning to propel himself without crashing. Following the others through tubes in single file, he arrived at a room with bolted down seats.

"Take a seat and strap down," intoned an attendant at the round entrance. "Take a seat and strap down." A brisk air flow through the low-ceilinged space helped forestall claustrophobia.

No sign of Ran anywhere; he couldn't possibly be healed from those burns yet. Spotting a dejected figure already strapped into a seat, Pel worked over to strap down next to her. "Hallie!"

Her eyes brightened. She reached out. "Pel. They can't do this to us." She spoke in a flat voice, without intonation.

He gripped her hand. "Except they have. Tell me what happened to you."

"They drugged me. I can't feel anything, not really, not inside."

"What do you remember?"

"I woke up in the hospital. My whole family was there. Mom was having a fit. I thought I had some dreadful disease. The back of my head was sore. I couldn't remember any reason for it. Then Security came to ask me what happened, but I was all confused."

Aryn floated over to strap down on the other side of Hallie. Pel nodded at her.

"Then the nurse came back in," Hallie continued in her monotone, "and said I showed Doramnis in my blood and that was why I couldn't remember anything. They kept me overnight in the hospital and sent me for a psychological profile to check that everything else in my brain worked, looking for *inimical* reactions, I think they said, to that stuff in my blood. I stayed in a small room and took their tests—brain scan, eyes, ears, everything. The psych tech said I was fit enough, aside from no memory for about twenty-four hours. I thought they'd let me go home, but they didn't. I got to attend classes, not live ones, but at least I wasn't falling behind."

"Welcome to Interstellar Ship Orpheus." A woman with captain's insignia loomed larger than life on the screen at the front of the room.

A man in turquoise with navy trim took her place. "I'm Eric Renal, ship's medico. You will be traveling in space sleep. Preparations for hibernation include both oral and inoculated medications to give you a comfortable journey. Your bodies will be kept several degrees cooler. Your hearts will beat very slowly. You will be in a state of torpor. Your body heat will periodically approach normal at which time you might have dreams, before once more cooling off and returning to torpor. You might become briefly aware of your surroundings. If you should rouse, have no fears. It is a normal process that keeps your bodies functioning at an optimal level."

Pel wondered if his nightmares would come back. Would he

dream of being engulfed by dark matter next? Probably not, now that he was living a nightmare. A wave of longing for home overwhelmed him.

His eyes rested on Hallie. How was *her* mother coping?

The medico continued. "You'll be monitored by sensors during the entire journey. In the unlikely event of problems, we will be aware. A few caveats now about your arrival. When you reawaken, you'll feel weak. Your strength will return as you resume normal activities. Also, when you awaken, you'll probably have little appetite, but it will be important for you to eat and drink frequently. And exercise. You may experience muscle pain. This, too, will dissipate with time and movement. Any questions?

"No? Then wait for your name to be called to be prepped for the journey."

Hallie mumbled, "I feel like I'm watching this girl who would be screaming if she could."

Pel tightened his grip on her hand. "I think we're being sent where my disappeareds went. Aryn here expects to find her parents."

"But why should they send *me* away? Liz said . . ."

"What did Liz say?" Pel asked.

"That she wouldn't stop them if she could."

What a strange thing for her sister to say. Beneath Hallie's lack of inflection, he sensed deep hurt. Fee-fi-fo. Volcano ready to blow. And he hadn't a clue what to do.

"Geoffrey Ramirez," called the attendant. A tall skinny teenager stood up with a grimace. Pel's ears pricked up. Ramirez? Geraldine Ramirez, maybe? He listened, hoping for but not hearing any other familiar names. Young people stood and exited as their names were called.

"Peleus Teague." The attendant's voice overrode Pel's thoughts.

"Oops, my turn." He squeezed Hallie's hand and released himself from his seat. "Help her, if you can?" He took Aryn's nod as agreement and fought queasiness to follow his guide.

Geraldine Ramirez. Sam Suzuki. *I'm on the right track. No going back.*

He turned. Both girls were watching him.

"Any questions about space sleep?" asked Medico Renal. The small compartment was lined with bunks, some occupied by the boys who had preceded him.

Pel, dressed in a one-piece, loose pajama garment, had swallowed innumerable tablets and lost count of the needle jabs. He shrugged. "I guess not, until I've experienced it."

"Anything worrying you?"

"Hallie Pollard. She's a friend. She's extremely . . . um unhappy about being here. If I can do anything to help her . . . I don't suppose it would help to complain to you about our, especially about Hallie's, being shipped out."

"Nope, 'fraid not. Thanks. I'll note you down as next of kin—so to speak. Get yourself comfortable."

Pel settled himself on his assigned bottom bunk. Not enclosed. It didn't feel like a coffin. Yet.

Hallie

P͟el disappeared. Hallie turned back to stare at the large screen showing a dark curve of the moon in shadow, with a scattering of stars.

"I wonder what we'll see when we wake," said the girl beside Hallie. Her smooth black hair fell in a graceful curve to her chin. How could she be so calm? She wasn't full of SereneAll.

Not yet asleep and already Hallie didn't want to wake. She had used to think she was smart, in a hurry to be independent. She cringed, remembering her mother's accusing look. Oh, *spam*. The drugs were wearing off.

Quick, think of something else. She was about to face space sleep, hibernation. Make a note to remember this moment. But when she attempted to record, she got only the thin buzz of no connection; the recording service was already out of reach. Instead, her voice burbled, "What a beautiful day!" She'd triggered an old entry, though she didn't recognize it. "I had so much fun talking with Pel—and watching both boys eat. Aunt Bet sure knows how to feed people."

The picnic had really happened! She hadn't thought to listen to her journal. She sounded so happy.

The girl next to her touched her arm. "I'm Aryn. Pel told me about what happened."

Happened. Hallie reached for her missing braid. If she could feel any emotion, she'd be envious of Aryn's hair and her calm. "It's as if I'm living in a . . . as if I've got a blanket wrapped around my head."

The official voice announced, "Haldis Pollard."

She fumbled at her seat fasteners, swallowing a cold dread that pierced the fuzz of her mind. Think of the courageous people in her life. Think of Pel, who'd left home to follow his mystery. Think of her sister, who ran a city. Liz always said, "One step at a time. You do what you have to do."

Hallie took one step. Then another.

oked, prodded, dosed, and dressed in a one-piece sleepsuit, she lay back on the assigned narrow bunk. The room held six bunks, three high on opposite walls. Above her two forms already lay still.

Pretend this is my bed at home, she instructed herself. She'd always listened to her day's journal entries. "A dream woke me," her voice spoke in her ear. An old entry from two nights after the bombing. "Those eyes. Like they were telling me something. Liz predicted I might have nightmares. But I want to know *why* it happened. The news report IDed the woman as some Congress rep's aide, called it a contract killing, and said it wasn't the first. They didn't even mention the banner."

Listening returned her to her tiny bedroom. She'd gotten up, opened her desk, and . . .

No! Don't think about that! Liz . . .

She backed the journal to find an older entry: "If I'm to be independent I have to act like it." *No again!* She had recorded that on the skybridge on the day of the bombing.

"Imagine! He's in tertiary with me. And I almost got him killed! I was in the middle of Dr. Wing's lecture when the bell rang. I thought I could just send him away without losing my connection. He kept ringing. And ringing."

That brought a smile. Dear Pel. He'd been so scared. And so brave.

Her body felt heavy, drowsy, the drugs for space sleep beginning to take effect, taking Hallie down and down. Her last waking thought was Liz.

She'd done something that made Liz angry.

Challenges

Ran

The speaker hissed on: "COMPARTMENT NOW ATTACHED. ALL SYSTEMS OPERATIVE."

What a difference no gravity made. For the first time since the explosion, Ran could move on his own. His bladder complaining, he fumbled with fastenings, careful to cling to the soft grips along walls, floor, and ceiling, all within reach. Only diagonally could he stretch out his arms and not touch a wall.

The tiny toilet compartment held no surprises. He had voraciously studied all details of space travel, but never considered what travel as a burn patient might be like, in that awkward gel pack. Afterward, he explored his tiny living space. Inside a storage slot was his bag of belongings and the minimal fittings of a virtual headband.

All that could wait. Exhausted, he reattached himself to his bunk. He was leaving Earth, leaving a messy trial, leaving Pel and Hallie and

181

the Sloans. What a backhanded way to get his wish to go into space.

The rumble of the ship coming to life woke him. He wanted to watch the Moon and Earth shrink away, but had no energy to look for viewscreen access.

They were speeding away. Just endure the pressure. Not so bad as the acceleration of leaving Earth.

I don't do virtual, he'd said. But his past came with him, no escaping it.

What else had he brought? Ran opened the storage slot. From his bag, he pulled out his favorite chess queen, rubbing it with his thumb. Mr. Carver who carved—a good joke to his six-year-old self—had left him the chess set, but the man had died. Then his foster family rejected him.

Had he been so unmanageable? Maybe. They'd used his visits to the old man as incentive for him to do his schoolwork. He'd been an outcast from the beginning, unable to participate in the school's virtual sessions, forcing his teachers to find alternative work for him.

He shoved his bag back into the slot and looked at the VR headband with distaste—an expandable band to fit around his forehead, with extruding contacts.

Coward, he jeered.

He pulled it on and stood upright. Water sparkled in sunlight. Arms reached upward, back and leg muscles contracted. A shallow dive. Water cool on blessedly whole skin. A piercing scream, followed by a roaring surge of terror! He was running, running to rescue Hallie.

Gasping, Ran yanked the contacts from his head, from water back to enclosing walls.

A long interval later, the door slid open. Renal's face peered in. "You okay?"

"I tried your blasted virtual. I told you it wouldn't work! How much damage did I do?"

"You were right about shorting out the system. What did you feel?"

"Panic."

"You'll have to look for the source of your panic, won't you?"

"A Jonah!" screeched a voice behind the medico. "A gremlin in the works. The last thing we need on this ship is someone who can wipe out the ship's brain."

"I did not!" said Ran. "Tell the brain to reconfigure the VR."

"In fact," added the medico, turning in the doorway to address the second voice, "if there's a way, set up a separate channel for his contacts, with instructions to reset every time he shuts it down."

"I'll talk to Captain. Don't let it go to his head. He'd better not get power mad."

"Who was that?" Ran asked. But the door slid shut, leaving him in angry silence.

$$\star \; \star \; \star \; \star \; \star$$

Seven meals into the trip, Ran was sick of it. He'd go space crazy long before they arrived at their destination—wherever in the galaxy *that* was. What was the point of leaving Earth to escape zombiehood? Being a zombie might even be preferable.

He slammed against the walls, ceiling, floor, trying to keep his body mobile, until his burning feet and back returned him to reason. The burning was painful but not like that weird time in the hospital . . . Ran gentled his exercise, crisscrossing his little cell over and over using ceiling and wall straps, remembering. Someone had come, shut off his pain meds, said nothing. The scanners showed nothing, but they tracked chips, not visuals. A mystery worthy of Pel. But Pel must be back in his village pursuing his tertiary studies.

To figure out time's passing, he could chart his meals on the walls like a prisoner. He flopped face down on his bunk. When his food slot pinged, he ignored it.

"Time to soak," came the medico's voice over the speaker.

"Leave me alone!" he snarled. No amount of medico cheer during a daily soak could change the rest of his hours. And no amount of being told to vex would make it work for him.

The door slid open. "I can't. You're my job."

There. He could keep track of time by the soaks. That first day—no, that first cycle—Renal had said, "Once every cycle you'll soak for an hour in the immersion tank while your suit gets recharged."

"Okay, do your job then," Ran said. He got up and entered the infirmary. Its larger space felt lighter, brighter. Out of the clumsy gel pack and into the immersion bath, almost as close fitting as his suit, but soothing to raw skin.

"And you learn to vex!" said Renal.

"I tried. It doesn't work. How many times do I have to tell you?"

"How many times have you tried it?"

"Three times a cycle. Then I quit. And this living in a sterile box is cruel and inhumane. Solitary confinement is defined as torture."

"What about your screen?"

"What screen?"

"All you have to do is say 'screen,'" said the medico.

"Doesn't work," said Ran. "You try it."

The medico stepped out and came back. "We'll have to get that fixed. No reason why you can't have access to info and entertainment. And figure out why it's not working."

Renal had returned to the subject of vexing. "I don't know why. All I do is make up stories."

"What stories do you tell yourself?"

"That someone put me in virtual when I was too young. It's been like that ever since I started school. Every time I put on a headband, I hear a scream."

"Memory. None of our vexing episodes includes a scream unless it's an animal or bird sound, and I think you can distinguish that. After your soak, I'll monitor you."

The medico got Ran back into his clammy gel pack. "I want you in here where I can request the ship's brain to continue the input even if you fight it."

Ran slowly pulled on the headband, waited for the contacts to extrude, and closed his eyes. Green grass. Trees. Like Hallie's park and that picnic. What a gorgeous day. A scream! That was Hallie! He was running to. . .

Blackness shut out the parkland. He reached hands to his head.

"Keep it on."

Ran opened his eyes on the infirmary. "I heard a scream."

"But it wasn't real, was it? Where were you?"

"A park with grass, trees."

"That's a gentle walk sequence. Builds up into a cross-country run if you stay with it. Try again. Interesting, how you exert such resistance."

Ran stared over Renal's shoulder at the wall, repeating silently: *The scream's not real. The scream's a memory.* He waited for the program to restart.

He walked along a path. A voice said, "Lilacs." He breathed in a sweet scent, passing bush after bush of white and varied shades of purple blossoms. He'd never known lilacs held such powerful sweetness.

"A scream!" Ran spoke aloud.

"Keep going," Renal said. "This is not real. Remember, it's all memory."

Bees buzzed greedily around the blossoms. The scream this time was accompanied by a blind, unreasoning panic. With a violent wrench of his mind, Ran broke free. He pulled the contacts off and wiped his forehead. "No! Enough." He headed for his own compartment.

"Your choice," said Renal. "If you can't take my word for it that you're safe, you'll have to work through it on your own. I'm as near as your speaker."

Ran shrugged. Nothing new about managing alone. Adrenaline still surged. He retrieved the meal from the wall slot. Ship food tasted hardly better than that at Workless. What he wouldn't give for one of Betty Sloan's meals. And for the peaceful work there. When would they fix his screen?

Try the headband again. Air chilled his cheeks. He glided on skates over ice. Music in the background, with a dancing rhythm. But then he was back in his cell. Eating hadn't been such a good idea. He threw the headband in its slot and flopped on his bunk.

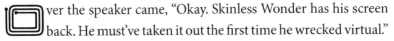ver the speaker came, "Okay. Skinless Wonder has his screen back. He must've taken it out the first time he wrecked virtual."

Skinless Wonder was he? The name-caller was back.

The medico peeked in. "Try calling up your screen."

Ran already had. "It works." He lost himself in possibilities. Index. Courses. Even a map of Orpheus's corridors.

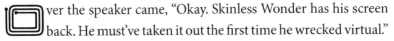omething woke him. The red glowing dot over his sliding door indicated the sleep cycle was still in effect. A faint scritching sound. Ran waved on the light, bringing the walls closer.

The scritching stopped.

On the floor beside him a small cleaning bot froze, programmed to work only while people slept. Then the cockroach shape backed away toward its wall slot.

Ran smiled and awkwardly leaned down to pick it up. "Hello, bot. Sorry to disturb you." He admired its structure, propulsion, and the fine bristles that swept miniscule debris into its expandable cavity. What air filters couldn't catch, the cleaning bots did. "Ouch!" He changed his grip so as not to contact the bot's digestive acids.

With a smart tool, he'd be able to explore its instructions. He set the bot on the floor and waved off the light so that it could return to work.

He was still smiling as he lay back down.

Awakenings

Ran

"Time to soak," announced Renal over the speaker.

Ran grimaced, not at the idea of immersion but at the ceaseless swamp of his suit. He'd lived in it for at least a month now, while the ship accelerated through the solar system.

The connecting door slid open and he went through.

"Spots are beginning to itch," Ran said.

"Healing," answered the medico.

"But there's no way to scratch."

"Good meditation technique, learning to ignore irritations," said Renal, rather unfeelingly.

"Am I taking up meditation too?"

"You have lots of time on your hands."

"I'd rather be doing," said Ran.

"You're making good progress growing muscle and skin,

considering the low grav. You'll be ready for doing, soon enough. Bones are another matter. Good thing you didn't break any. Your big challenge is learning to vex."

"Yeah, yeah. I'm working on it."

"How many attempts today?"

"Three. Takes a while to reconfigure."

"Tell yourself to dream about why. You had meditation instruction in school, didn't you?"

Ran nodded. "They called it Contemplation. I always cheated and talked to my desk."

"How is that cheating?"

"Teacher told us to empty our minds. Whenever I did, I heard the hum of my desk so I listened. I never got my mind empty."

"Machine guy, you say? Meditate on the ship's noises then. Can't hurt. Whatever takes your mind off the itch."

✶ ✶ ✶ ✶ ✶

Itching meant he was healing. Ran had settled into a schedule of classes, followed by abortive attempts to vex. Both occupations helped him forget his tiny quarters. Courses insisted on running sequentially. Impatient, he pushed himself to absorb as much as he could.

At Ran's next soaking, the medico said, "Soon we can begin to cut down on your suit. Your minor burns are healing nicely."

"If I'm healing, why can't I wear an exercise suit programmed to give resistance? Just give me a list of exercises. I'm not getting anywhere with vexing.

"But I'll keep at it," he added. A promise to the medico and to himself.

189

"If you'll keep trying to vex, I'll ask Second Mate Gumption to program an exercise suit for you with incremental increases in resistance."

"All right!" Ran relaxed as the bath took away the itches.

Vexing. The problem was that scream, and running to Hallie's rescue hoping to be in time . . .

But his block had begun long before Hallie. Someone else had screamed—so far into his past he had no memory. Something had caused utter panic. At least he could escape virtual. Not true for everyone. But he couldn't imagine a memory so horrible he refused to look. And, did he really want to know?

An exercise suit meant he could do resistance work.

Hallie

Hallie knew she was awake, but she couldn't open her eyes. Make it be all a dream. Let me go home, back to tertiary, back to the way it was. The ache in her throat, followed by waves of horror, said otherwise.

On a ship in the vastness of space, she was lost and cold, a meaningless speck. The past didn't matter.

But it did matter. The past would tell her why she was here, if she could only access it.

Hallie sank back into sleep, on her way to torpor.

"Now see what you've done!" said Liz. What had she done? Hallie only knew she had to run from something. She brushed past trees. The trees became clouds, then darkness. She ran past stars. Something chased her, no matter how far she went. She scooped up a small dog cowering on the street. Pel waved his arms, trying to hold back a cougar. The dog morphed into a cougar that spit and clawed until she dropped it. Pel still held his arms high, guarding her, but she passed him, unable to stop her flight. Thudding footsteps, breath hot on her neck.

The one behind drew closer. No escape . . .

Ran

Medico Renal fitted Ran into an abbreviated gel pack that enclosed only his torso. He guided medicated booties over still healing feet. Ran's feet were a constant reminder that he had been barefoot when he took off running across the park in response to Hallie's scream.

"These are for Skinless Wonder." That name-caller! Ran skidded around, saved from toppling by the medico's grab. A little man with pale reddish hair and deeply creased cheeks held limp tubes. "Humpty Dumpty, as I live and breathe."

Ran scowled. "Who're you?"

"Second Mate Gumption, at your service. Attach these sleeves when you're ready to exercise." He gave them to Renal and left.

"No time like the present," said the medico. "You've got your list of exercises."

Back in his little cubicle, Ran went to work, semi-content with this new challenge. But while gripping a ceiling loop, legs raised as though sitting on air, he paused. "That's not right."

He dropped the short distance to the floor. The sense of wrongness evaporated.

He'd been thinking of that little cleaning bot and, as always, listening to the ship's mechanical vibrations. He shook his head. Let the ship's brain sort it out.

Standing reminded him of his itchy feet. He completed his exercises, sighed, and reached for the headband. Time to irritate the ship's brain the way the second mate irritated him. With a deep breath, he brought his awareness to the ship's machines, and reached deep into that calm before setting the contacts in place.

Sunlight sparkled on water. He dove into the cool wetness, came up, took a breath, kicked his legs, stroked forward to complete a lap. Sun warmed his shoulders. Under the water, he listened to the splash and gurgle of circulating pumps.

Something still wasn't right and it wasn't pool noises. He swam another lap.

There. He identified the source. With huge regret, he slipped himself out of virtual and pulled off the contacts. Walls whirled as he shifted back to his tiny space.

"Engineering!"

"Gumption here. What?" That clown again.

"Something's wrong with a hydroponics pump." Ran banged his fist against the wall. They wouldn't believe him. And he'd vexed. He'd stopped a perfectly good vexing for this.

He pulled the headband back on. In the park walking through trees, but before he got to the lilacs, screams brought heart-thumping panic. His brain wrenched him free.

Blackout. Again.

Ran gave up and called up his screen for World History, which would be followed by biology. Periodically he tried to vex. He finally pulled on exercise sleeves and drove his body to its limits.

Pel

Cold, unable to open his eyes, Pel tried to work it out.

On a ship. *The Orpheus*. Orpheus went into the underworld in pursuit of his love. That made space his own underworld where he pursued answers. *But where were they going?* Those headlines that had appeared right before Turner collected him and delivered him to the spaceport—they *had* to be related to his question to the NODE.

"Mr. Teague."

A voice kept dragging him out of his thoughts. He tried to open his eyes, caught a blurred head with his right eye. He closed it and concentrated on lifting the heavier left lid. He didn't want to cheat by using his hands. This time both eyes opened slightly.

"My name is Teague, not *Teag-you*."

"Good. You are conscious and aware."

"So?" He shut his eyes, disgruntled. What rhymed with *gruntled*? Quadripuntaled. But he couldn't remember what it meant.

The voice again. "We need you to awaken, Mr. Teague."

Pel opened bleary eyes. "The medico. That's you." His eyes closed. "Are we there yet?"

"No, Mr. Teague. We're still accelerating through the solar system. You asked to be entered as next of kin to Ms. Pollard."

"Hallie?" His eyes opened more widely. "What's wrong?"

"She's physically fine. She's been having some nightmares, possibly due to the slow dissipation of drugs they had her on before she boarded."

"Or the Doramnis."

"Doramnis?" the medico repeated.

Memory flooded into Pel's fuzzy brain. "It was used on her in an attack a couple of weeks before we were shipped."

"Oh? That wasn't noted in my records. It has a slow half-life. At any rate, we decided a little awake time, and the comfort of a familiar voice, might help her process her nightmares."

"I'm the comfort part then. I don't recall any dreams."

"She may not either, but it's important that she receive reassurance before she sleeps again."

Pel shivered and tried to move.

"Easy. Don't exert yourself. We have to get your body warmed up first. Drink this."

A straw poked into his mouth and he sucked in something warm and sweet.

He followed the medico a short way down the hall where Hallie, wrapped in a blanket, huddled in a small cubicle beside a woman with short curly hair. From their first meeting, when he'd screamed at her to get out of the street, he'd felt a need to protect her.

He still did.

Counsel

Ran

The tap at Ran's door came hours after his call to Engineering.

"Second Mate Gumption, reporting." The little man wedged himself in the doorway, his back against one side of the frame, feet up the other. "'Check it out,' says Captain, so I check it out. How'd you do it, Skinless? Ship's brain shows you stopped vexing cold. Then you tell us something's wrong and identify the source."

Ran waved his screen off. "Still calling names, I see."

"What? You want me to pick on someone my own size?"

"You called me a Jonah last time. I'm a fixer. Machines are my skill—except for VR."

"No more Jonah. I'll stick to Skinless Wonder. You grow skin, you can be Wonder Boy."

Ran couldn't control a half grin. "Something had bothered me earlier, but it wasn't until I was vexing—swimming—that I heard it again and identified it."

"You couldn't have heard the hydroponics pump."

"Maybe heard isn't the right word, but hearing, listening, is what I call it."

"Huh." The little man used the doorway to do a handstand. Back upright, he said, "Meditate on hydroponics all you want. We need it for food, water, air, even you, Dead Weight."

"So, is everything okay with the pump now?"

"Time will tell. Why do you ask?"

"I don't know. I guess it's not my business." Except that they were all on the ship together. Ran pulled himself up using a ceiling loop.

"You made it your business before." Gumption curled up in the doorway again.

"An impulse. I didn't stop to think. You going to find a new name for me?"

"Like Skinless Impulse? Nah. You gave a genuine warning."

"I won't be growing skin forever. Is there . . ." Ran dropped to the floor. "Oh, forget it."

"You want to take over flying this collection of boxes?"

"I couldn't fly a ship to save my life, but I always wanted . . ."

"You'll have to keep yourself busy, Skinless."

"So where are we headed?"

"Polaris sector. Once we hit the hyperspace nexus, we'll really move, following the sequence mapped out by AstroMining. I hope they haven't steered us wrong. We take on precious human cargo— no one wants to be steered wrong."

"What human cargo?"

"Aren't you one of them? Why are you here?"

"Don't know, do I? No one's told me. I feel like a pawn in some cosmic chess game—thrust out in front to see what hits me. Isn't colonization against Earth regs? Is this some kind of prison planet we're going to? To be worked to death in mines?"

"I doubt that's why we're transporting kids, Skinless."

"Kids?" Must be true, what Renal had said.

"Kids like you. Returning them to their parents. Now why the parents are there . . ." Gumption shrugged. "Government ordered return of kids, with the specs to find the place."

"Government or NODE?"

"Same difference. But it wasn't NODE that stole people away—that was Atlas under the guise of AstroMining. Out of sight, out of mind. No skin off their backs. Heh, sorry! Anyway, that was their view, till they got caught."

"Wait a minute. Who do you work for?"

"Space Corps." And Gumption was gone. Space Corps? Sometimes called Space Cops; closest thing to Peacers outside the solar system. Except, they never carried passengers. How strange.

Ran settled on his bunk, considering Gumption's information. *Kids like you*, he'd said. Not like him. He didn't have any parents. Period. But Pel had associated fosterlings with his mystery—was this journey the NODE's answer to Pel's question?

So much to consider. He'd gone from swimming to identifying that noise to Gumption's information. He had chosen to slip out of virtual. No panic. His next job would be to find a way to stay in. Meanwhile—

Ran went back to exercising.

Hallie

allie realized she'd been dreaming when a soft voice woke her. She didn't want to wake. She didn't want to feel. Feelings were explosive—like body bombs.

"Sit up. Let's wrap you in this." Warmth enveloped Hallie but didn't dispel the chill. She opened her eyes.

"I'm Lieutenant Melissa Haight. You were dreaming. A nightmare." The woman wore turquoise with navy trim. She had warm, tawny eyes, her curly hair tinged with gray.

Hallie's dream fragments broke into smaller pieces, but she could recall no falling body. At least it hadn't been a replay of that sky-bridge incident.

"You're all right," said the lieutenant.

But she wasn't. She was on a starship, speeding away from home. She grimaced, swallowing hard.

"Come with me." With the woman's hand on her arm, Hallie shuffled down a passageway, the low gravity causing her steps to bounce. They entered a small room.

"Sit here." Hallie sat, tempted to curl into a tiny ball. She had never wanted to go into space. With a slight bustling at the doorway, the medico who'd talked about hibernation led Pel in. Pel looked as miserable as she felt. Without thought, her hand raised, reached for him.

"I've brought a friend," the medico said. "This awakening is purely temporary. I apologize, but you were under the influence of tranquilizing drugs when you went to sleep. We want to give you a chance to consciously process anything that might continue to bother you."

Pel sat down beside her, shivering. She pulled her wrap over his shoulder.

Pel

Hallie's gesture warmed Pel more than the shared blanket.

"Pel, where are we?"

"I don't know. The medico said we're still accelerating outward. That right, Lieutenant?"

"I'm Melissa Haight," the woman said. "And we're somewhere mid-solar system. We're sorry to disturb you two. Waking's the hardest part of ship sleep. We've only a short window of time before we have to put you both under again—say twenty minutes to half an hour—so don't expect to begin feeling comfortable. Mr. Teague, please talk with Ms. Pollard, and help her gain some confidence that all is well."

But all wasn't well. Turner had delivered him to the shuttle. Turner, the message bearer, with no explanations. Pel's head ached. Even after that drink, his mouth felt dry. His joints creaked. Why'd they have to exile Hallie? He didn't know how he was to help her.

He took her hand. A handholder, out in the colder world of ships and rips in time. Hallie returned his clasp. "What did you dream?" he asked.

"Something chasing me. It's gone now." She shuddered. "I'm cold."

"Me too." Pel moved closer. "Maybe the part of your mind that got wiped out by Doramnis is trying to recover. You must have experienced a real nightmare in the park. Can you remember anything?"

She pulled the blanket closer. "Liz was in my dream. She said, 'Now see what you've done!'"

Pel backtracked from thoughts of picnics. "Your sister was in your dream?"

"She told me to stop, when I researched those victims. And she told me again, when I was watching the plaza trying to figure out that Kansas for Kansans group."

He nodded.

"And . . ." Hallie's voice caught. "When they told me I was to be exiled, Liz said . . ." She swallowed hard and ducked her head.

Now it was coming—what she'd mentioned at Space Dock. Nightmares didn't arise out of nothing; he knew that from his own. He put his arm around her shoulders, waiting. They were both shivering. Orpheus had gone into the underworld for his Eurydice. Could that underworld have been as cold as this one?

"Liz said?"

Hallie muttered, "Liz said she wouldn't stop them from sending me, even if she could."

Pel's mind raced. "Why do you suppose she said that?" He'd never met Liz, but Hallie had talked of her as loving and tough and fair.

"She hates me."

"Nope. Try again. Why did she warn you from investigating?"

"Because they might use me to influence her."

"Could they have?"

"No. She'd have fought back."

"So . . . ? Think it through."

Hallie stirred. "So this is to protect me?"

"That's my guess. What a hellish choice for your sister."

Hallie sighed. "Maybe I can live with that." She snuggled closer.

Pel found her nearness distracting in spite of the hibernation drug's effects.

She took a deep breath. "Tell me about the picnic."

Pel shut his eyes, the better to pull up the past. "I arrived to find Ran working away on a model boat and you waiting with a picnic basket. We talked. And then Ran finally decided he was ready to go. Do you remember any of that?"

She shook her head. "Not really. Sort of. Maybe."

"I'll tell you everything that happened, except for the part that I don't know." And the parts he didn't want to remember. Why give her worse nightmares? "When you go back to sleep, keep telling yourself that you survived it. You're alive and well. You'll be all right."

She angled her head to eye him in disbelief.

"All right, I take that back. We don't know where we're going or what we'll find. But we will be together. And there are others. None of us knows what'll happen. So. The picnic. You chose a spot for us under a tree. The food was wonderful."

"What did we talk about?"

"We talked about Ran's boat, about our families, our classes, your investigations into the bombing, my mystery of disappeareds. You suggested Ran get a waiver to get him into tertiary. Oh, and something else. We started talking about Atlas Corporation. The disappearances occurred about the time of their final breakup. I mentioned that the last of the Dalguti family lives in Dodge. Ran and Jeb had made a delivery to a Mr. Dalguti—the same day I showed up at your aunt and uncle's."

"I helped Ran with that table," Hallie murmured. "And the arts guild won the Dalguti Prize for our Gilbert and Sullivan production."

"There. Full circle. We're all connected."

"But . . ." she said slowly, "Atlas. They were broken up. You think a remnant remains, still greedy for power?"

"Yeah, I think greed is alive and well. And who better than the family that headed up Atlas, clinging to what it was losing?"

She shivered. "Are they the reason we're being exiled?"

"I don't think so. They wouldn't be reuniting kids with parents, would they?" He hoped. There was still a possibility they were being disappeared like the ones on his list.

"I'm glad you're with me," Hallie said. "I wish I could remember that picnic. It sounds like fun." She relaxed even more, both of them leaning against the wall—bulkhead? or maybe that was only on oceangoing ships.

His arm tightened around her shoulders against the tremors running through them both.

"It was fun," he agreed. At first anyway. "I'm sorry I took a nap. I'd had so little sleep for the past week."

"Time to go." Medico Renal and Lieutenant Haight reappeared. "Thank you, Mr. Teague," said the medico.

"Don't forget," Pel said, giving Hallie a tired squeeze before removing his arm, "you're alive and well. I'll see you later."

"G'night," said Hallie. "Thanks."

He felt ready to topple.

"Back to bed," said the medico.

Pel stumbled. This time his bunk did resemble a coffin but he didn't care. He was half-dead anyway. "Call me if she—"

"We will. Sleep now." Pel hardly registered the cool injection. He didn't need it at all. So tired . . . But torpor didn't come instantly. He thought again of those headlines: AstroMining. Breathable Planet. And right afterward . . . exiled.

Cold crept through Pel's body. Back down into the underworld. Hallie. And his mystery—somewhere out there.

Hallie

Hallie shuffled back down the corridor. She'd been so conscious of Pel's arm around her, their closeness felt so right.

"I'm sorry we had to disturb you," said Lieutenant Haight. "It'll take you a while to resume space sleep. Breathe deeply. Stay calm."

Liz wanted to protect her. If she could only believe that. Her mistake had been in declaring independence, which allowed that legal writ to proceed. She hadn't gotten anywhere with her research and then she'd blown Liz into a huge tragedy. Stupid, stupid . . .

Or was she? After the accident at the park, when she woke in the hospital, she'd never seen Jeb so furious. Maybe someone had already threatened to use her against Liz.

Accident. She stiffened. Pel hadn't said anything about the explosion. She still didn't know what happened. Cold began to penetrate her body. Breathe slowly. Sleep.

Her body jerked the way it did sometimes when falling into sleep. But she could still feel Pel's arm holding her.

Ran

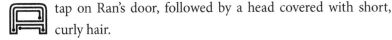

A tap on Ran's door, followed by a head covered with short, curly hair.

"Who are you?" Wearing the resistance sleeves, he got up from

his push-ups, conscious of his Humpty Dumpty look.

"You're a tall drink of water, aren't you? Melissa Haight, chief hydroponics officer, and med tech. I sometimes cover for Eric Renal. I just stopped to say thanks for the heads up on the pump. You let us know before it actually stopped. That's impressive!" She gave a nod and his door slid shut.

Ran swung around his cubicle by the ceiling straps. Another crew member considered him human. On his next loop around, he remembered he had messages. Handed to him by a different med tech weeks ago. He pulled his bag out of its cubby.

The small disc in his hand, he hesitated, then thumbed it on.

In the ensuing hologram, John Sloan's wild white hair flared around his face. "Ran, my boy." His voice carried Ran back to the workroom, its smells of woods and oils. "We learn by doing. Every generation in crisis learns firsthand who they can depend upon, who they can trust. My generation learned not only who to trust but also how to discover the trustworthy. You are one, and never forget it. We hold no blame for you in this tragedy, though with your strong sense of responsibility, I'm afraid you might be blaming yourself."

Ran's hand—and the hologram—shook. He blinked hard.

"But there's another lesson we learned, and that's to trust life. If you're doing your best, you can handle everything that life throws at you. There is a purpose in whatever happens. You have rare gifts and I trust you not to misuse them.

"No telling how many years Betty and I have yet to live. We hope to see or hear from you again. For now, take with you our love, and our belief that you will succeed in your quest, wherever life takes you. Believe in yourself, my boy." John's face faded away.

Ran's cubicle door slid open. Gumption folded himself into the opening.

Ran spun around; his trajectory bounced him off the opposite wall. He wiped his cheeks. "Why can't you knock?"

"I did." Glancing at the floor, Gumption said helpfully, "You dropped your message disc."

Ran bent to pick it up. "It was in my things," he muttered. "I hadn't listened to it yet."

"Yeah, people who care can do that to you."

Do what, bring him to tears? Ran scowled. "How d' you know? What good is caring, anyway? They're not here. You can't depend on people, ever."

"The human condition is essentially a lonely one."

Gumption had that right. "So why did you come?"

"I noticed you started studying geology. There are VR learning tapes that supplement that geology course. If you can swim and voluntarily break out, maybe you can figure out how to stay in a geology lab." Gumption unfolded himself and the door slid shut again.

Ran pulled out his bunk and threw himself down. More challenges. True, geology was dry stuff. VR would make all the difference. Once he conquered virtual, he could really get into that learning business.

John's message disc was still in his hand. Ran got up and emptied the bag on his bunk. His spare sandals—not the ones left at the park. His gray coverall from Workless, his tan street wear from the Sloans. He replaced the chess set and clothes back in the cubby.

Remaining on his bunk was a *second* message disc. And a small package.

The encircling plastic opened to reveal his knife and that unlucky smart tool. Unlucky or no, its fat pen shape fit his hand. Now he could examine the cleaning bot more closely.

Then he noticed writing on the wrapper:

Your friend Ty gave us an eyewitness account. He also told me of your smart tool fiasco. I asked your lawyer to claim it. Seemed only fair. I like the irony of a direflier tool going to a direflier destroyer. Jeb

Ran snorted. *There* was an irony, if this tool had created the very direflier he'd destroyed. Why not? If that labor pirate was mixed up with kidnappers but—*sheesh!*—where did it end?

A postscript in a different hand read:

Wish I could have halted that writ. Counsel Nagel

Having no pockets, Ran tucked the smart tool, knife, and note back into the corner of his bag. Strange to think of Jeb and Nagel getting together.

The second message disc still waited. With a deep breath, he thumbed it on.

Betty Sloan's face wavered before him. "Ran, my dear. Be well. Thank you for rescuing and protecting Hallie. Wherever you go, remember you have a place in our family. Never forget that." Her eyes narrowed in concern. "Take care of yourself. May life guide you well."

Ran stared at the empty space where Betty's face had been. Family? Too late. He gently tucked both discs back into his bag. A short message like that would last through several replays.

Too much, too fast. He had to move. He worked through all the exercises the medico had set up, then invented a few more.

Tired, he rummaged for the plastic wrapper and studied Jeb's words. Eyewitness account? Typhus must have been at the park, wearing his cloaking device. Creepy, the idea of someone watching them. Though how different was that from always being monitored by chip?

The first time he'd met Typhus, the vibrations of Ty's cloak had spooked him out of the alley and into the street. But he hadn't sensed anything at the park. Ty must have been at a distance. Who had set him to watching? And Pel had said he was being watched. Weirder and weirder.

But he had his smart tool back. Maybe it wasn't so unlucky. Tonight he'd catch that bot and have some fun with it.

He reached for the headband. Time to vex. He'd listen to the ship's noises. Bring on the panic.

Hyperspace

Ran

Ran had wasted almost three months trying to vex. Some virtual experiences now lasted longer than others. It all depended on how well he clung to his *listening*—but he had never yet reached the end of any VR program. Not even his attempts at geology lab.

Renal was threatening space sleep—like *soon*.

"TEN MINUTES UNTIL HYPERSPACE."

At the announcement, Ran tucked the cleaning bot into his storage compartment, along with the smart tool he'd been testing it with.

Renal tapped on his door and looked in. "Take care of all your physical needs, then strap down and stay there."

Curious, Ran settled on his bunk. Science still hadn't completely explained hyperspace. Everyone's reaction was said to be different. Even perception of time varied. But without hyperspace, that mainstay of old science fiction novels, travel between stars would require centuries.

He felt a faint nausea, heard an odd noise—not a ringing, not the familiar machine hum--this was almost a singing sound. So far, tolerable.

Except for in his mind. Faces, machines, school—like staring at a film of his life.

The other four-year-olds laughed and pointed at something Ran couldn't see. He'd gotten one quick glimpse of a funny clown before everything stopped. An hour later, the kids put on their VR headbands again. All but Ran. His teacher set a sheet of paper in front of him. "This says red," she told him. He already knew that. "Color the ball red." Obediently he picked up the red crayon, but his lower lip stuck out. When he grew up, he was going to invent a virtual that didn't scream at him, so he could have fun watching clowns too.

Five-year-old Ran rushed home from school. Today was the day he and Mr. Carver next door were going to polish the wooden chess pieces Mr. Carver had made for him. Then they would play a real game of chess—not just a practice one. He trotted down the hall towards his foster family's apartment, ready to wave when he passed Mr. Carver's open door. But his door wasn't. Open. Mr. Carver always always had his door open.

Ran's throat clenched. Too real, that last memory. People couldn't be trusted to stay. Without Mr. Carver to use as a bribe to do his homework, his foster parents had given him up, followed by another set before Doug and Marge took him on.

You're not my father. He remembered yelling that at Doug and at previous foster fathers. A wave of shame hit him. He'd left Doug, not the other way around. Doug had stuck by him. And Mr. Carver couldn't help dying. He'd decided to trust machines instead of humans, but even machines died eventually.

Machines—

He should have freed the little cleaning bot before lying down. Ran waved on his light and was immediately sorry. Walls too close, light too bright. He unstrapped and sat up. A wave of nausea hit. He pulled out the cleaning bot and lay back down. Placed on the floor, the bot sat motionless. Ran picked it up again and waved off the light. He stroked the back of the bot and shut his eyes. The whole ship was in pause mode until its return to real space. Nothing to do but wait.

✱ ✱ ✱ ✱ ✱

Workless's doors would be open. Hungry, Ran headed back at a trot. He opted for the shortcut through the last stinking alley—noid territory. Holding his breath, he speeded through. Near the far end, a vibration brought his neck hairs up. He dashed into the open street.

"Wheeet!" came a shrill whistle from the alley. Then a whisper. "You the Fixer?"

Ran stared until he spotted movement. He could just make out an outline—a small kid, cloaked. He had been sensing the cloak's vibrations.

He relaxed. "Yeah, I'm Ran. How'd you know me? Who're you?"

"My UncLum pointed you out. I am Typhus. Clan needs you to fix something."

"What 've you got then?"

"Vita-med fab. It be for my mother." He couldn't see the boy's features, but the boy's voice shook with desperation.

A repair. "I don't have much time." Ran moved back to the alleyway.

The fab's smooth ceramic base came into his hand with a friendly weight. Most households owned them, but Ran was surprised to learn that noids did too. This fab came with a recessed groove on top where miniaturized sensors tested a finger before it manufactured the supplemental nutrients.

"A smart one," Ran whispered to the fab. "I can tell you're a hard worker. Something must be blocked." He pressed the display button. Nothing. "I wish I had a smart tool to talk to you with." Instead, he pulled out his old combo blade. With the flat edge, he triggered the hologram readout.

"It wouldn't talk to us!" Typhus's voice rose.

Ran carefully read the message. "Now it will. It's clearing itself," he said. "It's old. Sometimes they need a little attention. It seems to have had good care. Be sure to keep the fluid levels high."

"We has lots of people can jam a scanner, but no one could fix this. Could you teach me to be a fixer?"

The boy's yearning reminded Ran of himself. "I don't know." Ran shook his head. "No one taught me." His next words came out of nowhere. "I just love them, see? They're not like people. They don't let you down, the smart ones especially. Tell it . . . Tell it thanks. Appreciate it."

A change in the boy's vibration caught Ran's ear.

"Here." He handed back the fab. "Your cloak power's getting low. If the fab doesn't clear itself, whistle for me again, okay?" He'd never talked to a noid before. Hurrying back to Workless, he wondered what had made him talk about love like that?

✳ ✳ ✳ ✳ ✳

an opened his eyes to the close darkness of his compartment. That word love had embarrassed him. Ty obviously loved his mother. It must be wonderful to have real parents. John Sloan had spoken of love. And Betty Sloan said he was part of their family. Others like Coach had stood by him. He'd left them all behind.

The *Orpheus* hurtled along in a different dimension. How unbelievably fast space travel had evolved. What those early explorers must have gone through. Amazing that any of them ever found their way back home to tell about it. Trust the ship. Love the ship's machinery.

Hallie

allie shivered a little as the dream state brought her closer to consciousness, closer to memory. Her filmy, flowing gown wasn't nearly warm enough but she had to be brave. Her striped hair flowed over her shoulders. As Iolanthe, she was prepared to face her doom, about to break her vow of silence.

"And I polished up the handle of the big front door," Pel sang.

"Oh, did you do *Pinafore* in the village?" she asked him as she leaned back on her elbows in the park. Pel and Ran were still eating. The picnic was a definite success, food-wise.

"We read them all, and did bits and pieces. Not enough of us for a production. What did you do?"

"*Iolanthe*," she answered.

"Hallie had the lead," Ran put in. "Silly stuff."

"Yes, I played a seventeen-year-old fairy with a twenty-five-year-old son." Hallie laughed. "But Iolanthe didn't do much singing."

"All the best lines went to the men," said Pel. "Like in *H.M.S. Pinafore*. 'I am the monarch of the seas, the ruler of the queen's navee' ..."

And then all three were singing, "And I polished up the handle of the big front door."

She was traveling, wasn't she? Toward tertiary orientation.

No, she remembered moving to Aunt Bet's. Where was she now?

Pel

Pel floated up out of torpor, thoughts sifting through North American history leading up to his disappearances. Those cyclical epidemic years of the Zank virus—the cause of that nasty unstoppable purging of bodily liquids. Next came Yucatan fever. As fast as science found a cure, a new disease erupted. Bodies all over the place. The Silent Years, when Atlas pulled the plug on communications. The thought police. The J'burg flu. And ...

He sank into REM sleep. The village tornado alert siren blasted.

Time to move into the shelter, but his legs wouldn't budge. The tornado came closer. And closer. Its cloud roared and swirled. It was full of objects. Credits. He knew they were credits, though credits had no physical form. The cloud spun. Quadrillions of credits. The spiraling money came nearer and nearer.

It swallowed him. Inside the tornado he found Ran. And Hallie. And the teens returning to their parents. A card flew past. He caught it. *Follow the money*, it read. A dark-haired guy grabbed the card and jumped into a direflier.

Alone, Pel stood on the prairie. The tornado roared past; Pel jumped on his bicycle to chase after it.

Metal Lollipops

Ran

"LEAVING HYPERSPACE."

Familiar sensations returned. Ran set the cleaning bot on the floor and watched it creep into its wall slot.

Using the smart tool, he'd discovered the bot's basic instructions to clean or call for help for larger messes, and some others. Simple instructions, like habits, were hardest to erase, not that he wanted to erase the bot's, but he wished he had a clue how to erase whatever caused his younger self to panic at virtual.

Best to try vexing before eating. Ran pulled on the headband and waited, holding fast to his love of the ship.

He *swam*, his arms pulled him forward, legs kicked, air bubbled out of his nostrils, head turned to gasp lungs full again. No itchy feet, what relief. Water washed over his bare back. Through one moment of panic Ran swam, soothed by ship's sounds. He swam until water

215

and pool faded into gray. His room shaped itself around him.

His breath had speeded up, body and muscles were warm and vibrant. *Finally!* Could he repeat that?

He collected his meal and ate, then called up the first geology field trip. Before affixing the contacts, Ran paused to ground himself in the ship's machinery.

Blue sky. The sun beat down on his back but a brimmed hat shaded his eyes as he examined the smooth surface of a feldspar shard and observed stratification of a rocky cliff. When the canyon excursion came to its natural end, Ran barely registered the close walls of his room, his mind full of possibilities.

"Time for your bath," said Renal over his speaker.

Ran stepped out, grinning wide. "I did it! I wanted to swim. I *did* swim. And no blacking out. And then I completed a geology field trip."

"Congratulations. Have you learned any more about why you had a block?"

Ran shook his head. "Hyperspace brought a lot of memories, but nothing that far back."

During his soak, he returned his attention to the ship. Something still nagged, but not like his knowing about the clogged pump. This was different.

Meanwhile, he'd finish that geology course and officially start tertiary. And vex—a lot. Build up bones and muscles. Once he was out of his gel suit, he'd claim Second Mate Gumption's promise of a ship tour.

✳ ✳ ✳ ✳ ✳

H e had joked with Pel about VR's addictive factor, but in him vexing woke an awareness and a craving for the Earth he'd left behind. Most of all he longed to reach the top of that mountain. He trudged, heavy pack on his back, snaking up an alpine slope, rocky peaks on all sides. A voice occasionally informed him of passing objects. "Alpine aster," as his eyes passed over a little purple flower. "Marmot," at the flash of a rodent's tail.

But halfway up that long, steep alpine meadow, the mountain turned gray. The ship's brain, monitoring his body, decided he'd had enough. He'd gotten hardly any farther than last time. In fury, he threw the headband against the wall. He had to see that view. Vexing worked. Only his body stopped him now.

He wanted to see from the top of that mountain. He'd had enough of being shut out of everything. Pel's voice sounded in his mind: *Horizons are in the mind, my child.*

Oh, that again. Horizons. His whole life had lacked horizons. The ship screen's view of space didn't begin to convey the horizons that vexing did.

Time moved strangely on shipboard. His movements brought the lights on. Immobility turned them off. Meals appeared. He soaked an hour in Medico Renal's presence. He ate, studied, vexed, ate again.

After that Colorado sky, his cubbyhole felt—and was—dingy, gray, and viewless, lacking the cumulus clouds, the cool air full of scents he couldn't identify. He wanted them back.

Hmm. He was beginning to see how people got addicted to virtual. Someone escaping chronic pain might choose to live in virtual reality. Fortunately, VR contacts provided a two-way circuit with its computer source to track body care or to circumvent starving.

217

✳ ✳ ✳ ✳ ✳

"**Y**ou've some minor scarring—not too bad considering the severity of your burns. I declare you healed," said Renal, and issued him a set of ship knits.

Ran luxuriated in the soft turquoise fabric, without the crew's navy trim. He had pockets again. But back in his tiny room, he realized that, along with his cumbersome gel pack, he'd lost the daily hour spent under Renal's care.

Back to solitary confinement. Back to trying to get to the top of that mountain.

✳ ✳ ✳ ✳ ✳

A couple cycles later Gumption stuck his head in. "End of my shift. Came for a visit." He inclined his head toward the infirmary. "Come out."

Ran couldn't hold back his complaint. "Doesn't it make vexers crazy to be climbing a mountain and then return to the same old ship walls?"

"Vexing is a promise and a memory. Keeps Earth close," said Renal. "I've never gotten to the top of that mountain. They say the sequence goes all the way—but it's hours long."

"I'm going to do it," said Ran. "I wish I hadn't lost so much strength."

Gumption, as usual curled up in the doorway, said, "We've begun the deceleration into the star system. You'll need to work fast. But right now, Wonder Boy, it's time for your tour. You should be good for a long hike." His eyes narrowed. "And Melissa Haight wants your opinion in Hydroponics before you take off vexing again."

"Then something *is* wrong," Ran said. That nagging feeling he'd had.

"You got it. Let's go." The top of the second mate's head barely reached Ran's shoulder. The narrow corridors stretched out before them. Gumption waved a hand. "All decks are set up on a round. Lower deck for storage, vehicles, and propulsion. Upper deck Radiation Repulsion. We don't go there. Living quarters and Hydroponics all here middeck. In fact. . ."

A wide doorway slid open at their approach. "Honey, here's Wonder Boy."

"Ran, right? I'm Melissa. You've probably noticed our second mate has a penchant for nicknames. In Greek, my name means honey or bee."

She toured Ran past walls of plants. "This area we call the plantation. Its plants require diurnal sequencing, meaning they need day and night cycles."

He became aware of a buzzing, and discovered the source near some flowering plants. "Real bees?"

"Yes," she answered with a smile. "Genetically modified. Live ones actually work better than bots. The name *hydroponics* doesn't nearly cover all our responsibilities. We run filtration for the entire ship. Our plants, from algae on up, are responsible for cleaning and recycling air and water."

She led Ran down more aisles of greenery. "This is a favorite walk for crew. The lighting is beneficial for plants and humans alike. As are cabin lights, of course, but somehow light filtering through greenery is calming."

"It reminds me of vexing." Ran took in the greens, the scents. They climbed a ramp away from the greenery. Gurgling sounded from beneath the deck.

219

"What do you think?" She looked at him with eyebrows raised.

"Metal lollipops," was Ran's first thought.

Gumption, following behind, chuckled. "Close enough."

"A garden of lollipop sensors," Melissa agreed, but remained serious. "Beneath our feet are the tanks and pools circulating the water system. This particular group monitors the filters and filtration."

Ran walked up to one and touched its metallic, ridged face. It vibrated slightly. Working.

"I wanted to ask how you react to this one." Melissa pointed to the next sensor in line.

Something was different. Ran frowned and looked at her. "It's working harder. What has you concerned?"

"It's allowing too much acidic water into the next pool. Why doesn't it correct?"

"Is anything wrong with its basic instructions or with the filters?"

"Not that we've found. The next sensor in line is having to run its scrubbers longer. If it goes the way of this one, it will cease to recognize its parameters. If the acidity reaches the algae it'll stunt its growth. We've slowed the flow, but it's going to backup soon."

"Why can't the ship's brain reconfigure the sensor?"

"It finds no problem. That's what's worrisome. We can isolate this pool and shunt the flow around it, but we have to find the cause." She bit her lip. "Bottomline, if one sensor has gone bad, others may follow."

"And if that happens?"

"Our garbage will eventually back up to poison us all."

Ran recalled a recent lesson. "Like kidney failure."

"A ship's equivalent, yes. We have to find the root cause."

"Are the lollipops linked," Ran asked, "or are they separate entities doing similar related functions?"

"Mainly separate. Certainly, they are linked within the ship's brain."

"If we have a sick ship . . ." He stared at the lollipop. "The question is, does the ship have the correct specs, or have the specs themselves been altered—the way cancer alters a body's integrity by redesigning the instructions?"

"Good questions, Wonder Boy," said Gumption. "Inspired by those medical courses you're watching?"

Irritated, Ran made no answer, though unsurprised to know his every move was monitored. He headed off to visit each lollipop sensor in turn. A while later he returned to the problem sensor. Melissa and the second mate hadn't moved.

"Communing with them?" asked Gumption.

Annoying! The man reminded Ran of his last foster father, always watching and commenting. "Just . . . Yeah." He'd learned to block out Doug by focusing on machines, which had never stopped Doug from insisting on homework first. But there *was* a problem and he'd been aware of it for a long time

"That pump," he said, turning to Melissa. "The one I alerted you to, back before hyperspace. Did you discover what was wrong with it?"

"That was so long ago!" she said. "We ran a backwash, which seemed to clear it. No problems since."

"Any proximity to your sick sensor?"

"Ye-e-es, as a matter of fact." She lowered her voice. "Ship. Give me the hydro layout." A hologram hovered, mapping Hydroponics, including a moving flowchart.

Fascinated, Ran pored over its details. "Which pump?" She

pointed. "Which lollipop?" Her finger indicated. Could they be related?

The unspoken question hovered.

"I don't see how," she began. "There's been too much time between the blockage and this current problem."

"Ask," said Gumption.

She deepened her voice again. "Ship, when HP38 pump slowed down, what was the cause?"

"WORKING . . . FOREIGN BODY. UNKNOWN SUBSTANCE. TRAVELED THROUGH SUCCESSIVE UNITS TO LODGE IN HP38 PUMP."

"What became of the foreign body when we backwashed HP38 pump?"

"WORKING . . . BROKEN INTO SMALLER FRAGMENTS. PASSED THROUGH."

"How do we know it was harmless?" worried Melissa. "Smaller bits of it could infect the entire system."

"Ship's brain believes it to be harmless," said Gumption.

"It didn't say that. It said 'unknown substance,'" Melissa answered.

"Honey Bee, are you thinking this is contagious? Something infecting the sensors?"

"It's been a fear, yes. I came across reports of a similar problem in Interstellar *Goliath*. They arrived back at Earth on emergency air and water. Had to totally refit and reprogram from their brain on down."

Ran whistled amazement.

"Could *Goliath* have been sabotaged? Could this ship?" asked Melissa.

"Sabotaged? We have no way of knowing yet. But if we can't reverse these changes, we're in big trouble."

"Key is identifying what the substance is." Melissa stared down the length of the room, thinking. "If it's epigenetic, it's insidious."

"Cellular changes," Ran said. John Sloan had used the term epigenetic, too, about his early upbringing--a good kind of change. The Hydroponics problem was more like a cancer.

"Exactly," Melissa agreed. "Cellular instructions—how do we change them back?"

"We've got to shunt this off-line," said Gumption.

"Yes, but it's been far too many cycles since that stoppage! Whatever got in is probably now systemic. We've got to identify what happened and change it back."

Gumption deepened his voice. "Ship. Trace back to find the source of the foreign matter lodged in HP38 pump."

"WORKING . . ." After a long pause, "FOREIGN MATTER THAT BLOCKED PUMP HP38 ENTERED THROUGH SYSTEM CT38."

Grim-faced, Gumption said, "Ship, who uses CrewToilet38?"

"UNDERGARDENER BLAINE AND SECURITY CORPSMAN WEX."

"Ship, have Security detain both for questioning."

To Ran, Gumption said, "I'll see you back to your cell."

He moved so fast that Ran had to lengthen his stride to keep up. Gumption's rumbling question to the ship had triggered a memory

"It was you that first day. You moved me to my room, and didn't let me see you. Why was a second mate doing that kind of work?"

"We had your records. Cap'n wanted my impressions of you, Skinless. What kind of passenger was she letting on her ship—someone outside of hibernation? She doesn't take chances, I told you."

"What kind of impression could I make at a time like that?"

"Even reaction to pain tells a story. You weren't screaming, ranting, or raving. *Au contraire*, you were all attention to the ship. Of course, the worst psychopath might ignore pain—but I've learned to trust my gut instinct."

Whew! breathed Ran as his door slid shut. *I'll see you back to your cell.* He *was* a prisoner. But the ship had a problem and an enemy. And hydroponics was vital.

Ran called up the screen and set himself to learn what he could of hydroponics systems.

Early in the following cycle, a guard tapped on his door, interrupting Ran's first meal. "Lieutenant Haight requests your presence in Hydroponics."

He was still chewing when his escort presented him to Melissa, standing beside the troubled sensor.

"After you left, the acidity levels dropped a bit. No real reason to think you made a difference, but if you did, I want to use you."

Ran shook his head. "I've only felt that something isn't right," he confessed. "I don't know how to describe it—like it's running less smoothly, or working harder than the others."

"Whatever you did or didn't do, if you can keep them healthy, you help the ship. I've been urged to add a basic solution to bring the acidity down. It would help forestall the rise in CO_2, but it has problems of its own, inhibiting algae growth, for one.

"And I've been monitoring since you were here last. The acidity hasn't dropped more—but neither has it risen—so I wonder if you'll participate in an experiment and see if your presence makes a difference."

A man approached from the green plant area. "Lieutenant, you want me to carry on as usual or continue monitoring?" While they conferred, Ran looked over the other sensors. Machines to work with. He had a job at last.

Melissa returned. "So, would you continue visiting them?"

"Sure, but I don't know if I really help. Is it okay to use my smart tool?"

"What could it tell you?"

He shrugged, healed skin sliding smoothly under the ship knits. "It's old, probably lacks the specs to do anything." He pulled the smart tool out of his pocket and connected it to the troubled lollipop. The tool's light display flickered warm yellow with a tinge of red. "I was right, it's too old to give a reading, but it confirms the sensor *is* working hard, struggling even."

She pursed her lips. "Don't use your tool. I don't want Captain down my neck if anything else goes wrong. I'll show you how to read for acidity and the normal parameters. We still haven't identified the contents of that pellet, but Gumption got a strange tale from one of the crew."

"Yeah?" His curiosity went on alert.

Her mouth turned down. "Wex is one crew member who'll never again serve on a ship. But it's Gumption's story. You'll have to hear it from him."

"Can I visit all the sensors?" he asked. She nodded. "And in the gardens?"

"The plantation? Sure, feel free."

Ran continued on alone. Peaceful and real. Machines doing their jobs. Everything was set close together. More than once he brushed past a human worker. He saved the green plantation area for last. The stingless bumblebees were good company, purposefully going about their business. The plants and the sensors monitoring light and nutrients were alive in a way that vexing never could be, their scents reminding him of that mountain, which thought reminded him he needed exercise.

After completing the rounds, he returned to the problem lollipop, and located Melissa. "I need to go vex now. Can I come back?"

"I'll call an escort for you. Yes, I do want you back."

A different guard accompanied him to the infirmary. The door to the larger room slid open, and then his own. Locked in again—but he'd tasted freedom.

✷ ✷ ✷ ✷ ✷

Ran ate. Instead of the mountain, vexing produced a series of calisthenics for his upper body, followed by a brisk jog. As it ended, the speaker said, "YOU ARE WANTED IN HYDROPONICS."

His escort hurried him down the long curving corridor. Ran mounted the ramp, where Melissa met him with a worried look. "Thank you for coming," she said.

Surprised at her politeness, he said, "What's wrong?"

"The next two sensors seem to be in trouble. We're running a check of the pools, but the next in line are definitely acidic. We're afraid a genetic marker is slowly taking over."

Gumption mounted the ramp behind them. "Honey Bee here has decided she needs you with her sensors. No accounting for taste, Wonder Boy."

"Me?" Too many ifs. Too much he didn't know.

"She thinks you've got an empathy that transmits to machines and helps them work. You told me yourself you can fix anything."

"Sometimes I've known what I was doing," Ran protested. "This time I have no idea. I mean, I feel them working and I know if they're struggling, but . . ."

Melissa broke in. "No buts. You knew Hydroponics had a distressed pump before Hydroponics knew. You'll have to accept your own gift." She studied his face. "I have no idea what it is that you do, but they seem easier for your presence."

"What is going on?" Ran turned to Gumption. "What did you find out from those two crew members?"

"Not nearly enough!" said the second mate. "We have a gullible fool. Someone back on Earth said to Wex, 'You're shipping out? I've got a job for you. It won't damage the ship or your survival, but we need delays. Swallow this after takeoff.' The fool claims to have forgotten. When he remembered he had it, he flushed it. We're still wondering what it would have done if his body had broken it down first. It might have gotten a lot farther into the ship's system after being digested."

Ran shook his head. "Why sabotage? Who put him up to it?"

"He doesn't know, and right now the why is beyond us. Except . . ." Gumption paused in thought. "Cap'n is concerned that he comes from Dodge."

Ran felt a chill. "Why Dodge?"

"Why Dodge? Origin of that People First movement? Close to the capital? Who can say? Someone doesn't want us to arrive. Wex is lucky he didn't swallow that pellet—the way he swallowed their line. I bet he'd be dead already and no way to trace the source. Get it?"

Ran got it. "What about the other one?"

"What other one?"

"The other one using that crew toilet?"

227

Gumption hesitated. "Undergardener Blaine. He checks out."

"Why was Wex told to delay the ship?" The damage had potential for far more than that.

"Couldn't say. You coming or going?"

"I just got here." Ran put questions out of his mind and worked from one sensor to the next, *communing* with them, as Gumption termed it. The pH measurements didn't always gibe with their supposed range. It was like they were feverish, trying to shake off an infection.

He'd been sick once at Workless, right after he arrived. He'd waited outside all day, his mind muddled. Once the doors opened, Mukerji took one look and said, "You look ill, young sir." Ran had headed for his bed, uninterested in food. Mukerji caught his arm and he'd jerked away. Mukerji touched him again and Ran gave in. "Come this way first, young sir." Mukerji pulled him away from the stairway, through a door, and sat him down on a chair. The chair reclined. What a relief to be off his feet. He lay back and shut his eyes, enjoying the soft hum of the working chair. An hour later, the chair disgorged him, weak but clear headed, feeling wonderful. Mukerji had done for him what he wanted to do for these sensors, except he had no diagnostic chair. But Mukerji's empathy had acted on him first.

Who would mistreat a ship this way? People First was a widespread movement, even if it did begin in Dodge. So, who would profit by delaying or preventing the ship from arriving? Ran shook his head. He needed Pel's brain for that kind of thinking.

He caught sight of Gumption. Had he been there all along? Ran resumed the earlier conversation. "I don't see how anyone could be so stupid. Is Wex feeding you a line?"

Gumption said, "Instruments say not. I would agree with you, except the human ability to be stupid has been proved over and over again."

"Yeah, there is that," Ran agreed wearily. He didn't know why he felt so tired. He hadn't done much of anything.

"When did you last eat?" asked Melissa.

Ran shrugged. He remembered eating before vexing. He stretched his arms overhead. He needed more yoga; his back was stiff.

"Go eat," ordered Melissa. "And don't come back until you've rested and vexed."

Now that he thought about it, he was starving.

Back in his cell, a meal sat in its slot. He no sooner pulled it out than another popped in. He pulled the seals off both and breathed in their steamy odors. He would have eaten a third if it had been offered.

Vex or sleep? He lay down. First thing after a rest he'd . . . research . . .

Nightmares

Hallie

Hallie shivered as her dream state brought her closer to consciousness.

She strode along the park perimeter trail. She'd never known the park to be so quiet; even her footsteps made little noise.

"I don't see him anywhere." The voice out of nowhere brought her to a halt.

"We know he's here. Something's masking his chip." The second voice broadcast frustration. Both were male.

She stopped. They said "he" and "his."

In the shadows, half-hidden between trees and shrubbery, she glimpsed a gold head—one of those expensive, burnished 'dos using tiny amounts of real gold. The other had smooth, dark hair fastened at his neck. Beyond them something light caught a low sunbeam—a partially furled cloth, reminding her of that banner attached to the airboarder—

Terror struck like a splash of cold water. Turn around!

Relax. Why should she? She was halfway around the park. Just because she'd been talking to Pel and Ran about that skybridge bombing . . . They were looking for a he.

She walked steadily forward. Pretend she'd seen nothing, heard nothing. She was past them. Almost to where the trail turned following the irregular outlines of the park.

"She's one of them! Get the spray!"

Her feet didn't have to be told. She flew. Rounded the bend. Steps pounded behind her. The gold-headed one, his face masked, burst through bushes directly in front of her. He aimed a bulky gun. She turned to find the other blocking her way.

Hallie crashed through the shrubbery. Find a house, a person. "Help!" she shrieked.

Misty drops shrouded her, broadcasting some strange, medicinal odor. She tried not to breathe, but her legs grew heavy. She clung to a tree trunk, tried to pull herself around it. Her second cry for help sounded weaker to her own ears. Her arms gave way, and she stumbled forward, tripping over a cotoneaster, falling through its stiff branches onto sparse, unclipped grasses. She stared at a dandelion stem whose seeds had flown.

A voice said with satisfaction, "We'll use her instead."

Hallie's memory shifted to nightmare. She thrashed, trying to escape a mist with a strange odor. No, not strange. They called it Doramnis. She twisted away from the mist, but there was nowhere to go. She stood on an airboard flying toward a skybridge. Someone watched from the bridge. It was herself, screaming at herself to go down. They were using her against Liz, punishing Liz for not doing what they wanted.

Don't run into the bridge. Avoid it. She twisted and squirmed, trying to make the airboard obey. But below was nothing but black space. Stars.

She screamed.

"Wake up now."

But she was fine. She'd survived. Pel was with her. She could turn and look at the threat.

"Ms. Pollard, you need to wake up."

Hallie didn't want to wake. She turned to look at the two who were chasing her, to tell them what she thought of people who terrorized other people. Just as Liz would have done. What they were doing wasn't right. People deserved to live without fear.

Ran

Wearing the VR headband, Ran had climbed above the tree line. Ahead was the ridge. A hiker paused there to look out at the view. Another turned to the right and headed up a steep slope. Oh, he hadn't realized the peak was still higher. The clouds overhead had grown thicker. A drop of rain hit his cheek.

The mountains went on forever, stretching toward the horizon and the sky. He stood on the knife-edge of the ridge; below, the ground fell away abruptly. He wanted to gaze longer at that view with craggy peaks in all directions, but his virtual body turned him toward the next climb, a rounded slope entirely covered with loose rocks, as if the solid rock of the peak had crumbled to bits.

Ran's compartment walls closed in. He pulled off the headband with mixed feelings. His farthest yet! His legs ached. Next time he'd succeed.

Another meal waited for him. And he hadn't yet researched the ship's hydro system. Hungry, he collected his food.

"YOU ARE WANTED IN HYDROPONICS."

Ran's escort accompanied him down the now familiar corridors to Hydroponics. He paused a moment to rest his eyes on the greenery, then squeezed past a couple of workers to mount the ramp leading to the lollipop sensors. A crewman followed him up the ramp and bent over one of the instruments. Ran stopped to watch, and asked, "What are you doing?"

The man turned. "Measuring CO_2 content in the air. It's higher than we like to see. I'm Ensign Blaine, undergardener. You must be Lieutenant Haight's machine empath. She was called away but should be back soon."

Blaine was the other person in that compartment. Gumption had said he checked out.

Ran left to give the sensors all the encouragement he could muster up. *Lollipop, lollipop, what do you need?* The first one hummed with life; still, he felt its struggle.

He'd communed with most of the sensors by the time Melissa arrived, a deep wrinkle between her eyes, accompanied by the second mate. They called up a flickering holograph. Ran held back, unwilling to impose his ignorance on their conference.

At Gumption's inviting nod, he moved forward. "Turns out, after due consideration of all the facts, we've got a long-term escalating problem. That blockage merely alerted us to it," the second mate told him.

"We've replaced the algal filters several times," Melissa added. "Something is causing cellular changes in the algae within the filter. That results in less cleansing of CO_2, but we haven't located the source. Acidity levels have been on a slow rise almost since we left Earth. Since leaving hyperspace, they've really taken off. I thought your presence was slowing the acidity rates—and I can't prove otherwise—but we haven't found the source."

"So, Flatfoot, what do you think?" Gumption asked.

"Sounds biological and not the sensors' fault," said Ran.

"Loyal to your machines, I see," said Gumption.

The discussion became more technical and Ran wandered off to visit the remaining lollipops. If the filtration system failed, first the algae would die; oxygen levels would go down—sounded like they already were. The plants would go, if the same poison got to them. O_2 would decrease even more. Without the algae, plants alone couldn't keep up with the ship's oxygen needs. The ship, no doubt, held emergency O_2. Drinking water could be distilled—but, but, but . . .

The beautiful balance of life would be destroyed.

Possibly an hour later, raised voices alerted him that the conference was over. The tap of purposeful steps brought his head up.

Melissa's mouth was a firm line. "Is this yours?" She held his smart tool in her open palm. Ran stared. He felt his pocket.

"It must be. Where did it . . . "

"I thought I told you not to use it," she said sharply.

"I didn't," he protested. The machines were working hard, but the problem wasn't with them. Besides, he couldn't have done any damage with it—even if he'd wished to.

"You're going back to your room now," she said.

"What's going on?" he asked, but Melissa nodded curtly toward

Ship Security at the bottom of the ramp. Two of them, a man and a woman. Ran swallowed his questions and left.

Back in his cell, he faced confusion. First they requested help, then they suspected him of—of what? He hadn't used it! He hadn't even thought about his smart tool after Melissa said not to use it. He'd left it in his pocket.

He couldn't sit still. He grabbed the nearest of the hand grips on the ceiling and, legs tucked under, swung around and around the tiny room. Sent to his room like a kid! Under guard like a criminal!

Again and again, the nightmare of Melissa holding his smart tool in her hand. No, he hadn't used it on the ship. "NO!" he shouted to his walls.

They were wrong! Was it really his smart tool? He dropped down to search his cell, rummaged through his bag, knowing he hadn't put it back.

The ship would know. All they had to do was ask.

He went back to swinging, thinking. He'd called the problem to their attention. Now they blamed him. Someone needed a fall guy. Someone wanted to stop the ship's arrival, or to cripple it, or to take it over. Ensign Blaine had called him Melissa's machine empath. He'd spent hours bent over sensors, listening to their hums and their silent voices. Anyone could've taken it. Someone planted that evidence.

Melissa didn't say where she found it. First she needed him. Now she believed—

She was wrong!

His stomach burned. The ship could confirm his story and hadn't. The ship didn't care about him. Why should he care about it? He'd given it hours and hours. Time to escape and finish climbing that mountain.

He pulled on the headband, stepped onto the alpine meadow. His muscles worked smoothly, an easy climb in spite of the steepness.

But something felt off. Anxiety? No, a boiling, churning anger. Unlike other vexings, he didn't hear a scream, but his climb was over. He was back in his tiny cell staring at walls.

So, no escape. Do something, anything.

He pulled out the resistance sleeves and swung, banging into one wall after another. His whole life, his whole life one step forward and back—again, and again, and again. He dropped to the floor, walked across it on his hands, breathing heavily.

Who was he? A fixer. What made him a fixer? Loving machines.

Why did he love machines? They didn't fail him the way people failed him. He reversed his course to tiptoe across the ceiling. Machines hadn't failed him, but this time? This time, he'd slipped out of virtual. The secret had always been to listen to the ship.

He pulled his bunk out and forced himself to lie still. The ship had a job to do. No one had asked it about that smart tool. The ship hadn't betrayed him. Someone was out to betray the ship, poison its life support.

He was a fixer. He could go on being a fixer, listening—

But no one cared about him!

All right then, he had to take care of himself. Let the rest go. The hurt, the pain, the betrayals of that labor pirate and others, the loss of Pel and the Sloans and Hallie, the long-ago loss of parents—let them all rest somewhere else. His throat ached. For now, let them go.

He would care for the ship. He tuned his listening to the ship's workings.

That capsule or pellet had come from Dodge. He came from Dodge.

He got up. "Screen." He'd study hydroponics. Commune with the ship. He'd listen to it, love it, do what he could.

Pel

Pel had been hearing his name called over and over. He was getting tired of it.

"Mr. Teague." The medico's voice. The one whose name meant kidneys. Renal.

"Are we there yet?" He remembered asking that before.

"No, sorry. You're needed again. Getting close, though."

"Is Hallie all right? We have to stop meeting like this." Pel kept his eyes shut.

"She'll be fine. You're right. It's not healthy. This time we're letting you really wake up. We won't put you back into hibernation. But you'll have to obey ship's rules."

Pel shivered. "Whatever. It'll be worth it to get out of this iceberg."

He was going to see Hallie. Must be more nightmares. Maybe she remembered.

* * * * *

The female lieutenant was escorting Hallie out of her room as Pel staggered from the boys' hibernation chamber. Hallie gave him a half smile. They were ushered into the same empty chamber they'd sat in months before.

"I'll be with both of you shortly," said Medico Renal. He looked preoccupied.

"How long have we been travelling?" Pel asked the lieutenant.

"About five months." She frowned and tugged her ear. "Talk to each other. I've got to deal with a problem."

They settled on the bunk lowered for them to sit on. "How are you?" he asked Hallie.

She told him of being chased in her dreams. "Also, the smell of Doramnis. I don't know if that was just a dream thing or if I really did remember its scent."

"It'll come," said Pel. "Sounds like it's struggling to come out." He swallowed some of his hot drink, hoping to stop his inner tremors. Or maybe not stop them. The tremors were doing their job, trying to warm him up. Oh, to feel alive again.

The door slid open at the medico's tap. "Well now, you two look a little more awake. We'll arrange a couple of rooms for you for the remainder of the voyage. Because of our crew shortage, you will be restricted to those rooms, but it won't be for long. Furthermore, to combat the effects of ship sleep, I expect you both to eat all meals and exercise in virtual as much as possible to recondition your physical systems."

From outside the room, a voice said, "What are you doing?"

Pel straightened. "That's Ran's voice!"

The medico leaped up. "Stay here!"

Hallie looked at Pel, then got up to look out. "No one there."

Pel peered over her shoulder. A bee flew toward them, then veered away. "Bees on a ship?"

"They use bees for the plants in hydroponics. Pel, something's wrong." Hallie turned wide eyes on him. "They wouldn't let bees fly all over the ship. Hydroponics must not be sealed." She followed the bee down the passageway and around the bend.

They'd been told to stay. Pel sighed and went after her, in time to see the bee fly into an open doorway. "That's your sleeping room," he said. "I saw the lieutenant close that door."

Something was wrong. He followed Hallie and the bumblebee into the girls' hibernation room. A strong puff of wind from the room made him cough. In the center, between the rows of sleep containers, the bee slowly tumbled to the floor.

"It's dead." Hallie looked into the faces of her fellow travelers. "Pel, something's wrong! They're not breathing right." She took three steps back to the doorway and hit the red alarm button. A siren began to howl. The door slammed shut.

Pel was startled. How could she tell? Then he saw a girl's agonized expression through the sleep container's clear cover—that wasn't right.

Hallie opened the covers one after another. Additional alarms rang with each lid opened.

Pel's heart raced, struck by sudden terror. He gasped for breath. All that air coming in should make it easier to breathe, shouldn't it? He needed to check on the male sleepers, but the door wouldn't open. Hallie looked across at him, her face straining, one hand to her chest.

Oh crap, caught in a death trap. He tried to reach her.

He thought their hands met as she fell. And then he had no thoughts.

Escape

Ran

Lying in the dark, Ran could remember someone brushing by him while he leaned over a sensor, but the tool might have been taken at any time in those narrow plantation aisles. It changed nothing.

He waved on the light. "Screen."

He asked for flowcharts. Sooner or later that fluid from the hydroponics system would meet up with the potable water for the crew. The air flow chart showed a tangle of vents; each room module a sealed entity, with vents for fresh air and used air. The lungs of the ship depended on the plants to produce oxygen. Tracing the chart, he followed the routes: engineering, piloting, infirmary, hibernator units, individual sleep units . . .

The ship's brain was cyborg, both machine and organic, requiring air and nutrients, plus power from the ship's drive. All ship systems linked together, like a living body. Killing their water supply would deal a death blow to life systems, as well as cripple ship intelligence.

There were emergency reserves, but that supply would be limited.

Someone didn't want them to get where they were going.

Ran slammed a fist against the wall and felt it give—a reminder that his compartment was one more module, set on this particular hallway next to the infirmary.

A ship seemed a flimsy vessel to chart its way across space. He wanted it to arrive.

Melissa Haight said the acidity had been increasing since they left Earth. Ran thought it through. He called up a map of the ship. The split screen showed the passageways on each of the ship's levels, with Hydroponics in the center. His lollipops—he could almost feel them laboring. From memory he traced the progression of pools, algae to higher plants. He didn't see where . . .

Melissa or Gumption had pulled up that chart of crew toilets and asked about the source of that capsule. What if . . .

Ran paced. It was frustrating to pace in what amounted to a very small circle.

"Second Mate Gumption," he said abruptly to the speaker.

"What, Skinless?" Gumption sounded preoccupied, impatient.

"Two things," Ran said. "A ship needs dual and triple safeguards. What if this sabotage had at least a double safeguard? One person flushed a capsule. What if someone else swallowed one and continues to excrete this epigenetic stuff? And second," he talked fast, praying Gumption wouldn't cut him off, "if the sensors could be programmed to identify DNA, the way cleaning bots can, why can't they be set to identify the changes as they happen and . . ." Ran realized he didn't know enough about how to stop the changes.

"Good try, Skinless." The closed connection crashed against Ran's ears. Did Gumption think he made sense or was he being sarcastic?

"Gumption," he said again. This time there was no answer.

"Medico Renal," he tried. When Renal answered, Ran said, "Listen to me. I've been set up. Someone's trying to make the ship unlivable. You need to watch out!"

"I'm working on the problem and am available only in an emergency." Renal sounded distracted. The connection closed again.

So much for that effort. If the poison got into the drinking water, they'd all start excreting the stuff. Then what? Simple. There'd be no solution.

Wait! It might require a total wash of the system. But he didn't see how that could take place way out here. Maybe if they added another stop to block the flow—

No, whatever got through would be insidious and continue replicating. They needed the equivalent of an antibiotic—something to change the cells back to their former state.

Ran reached for his smart tool. He'd gotten used to holding it for comfort—the way Hallie reached for her long braid—but he found only his little knife. All right then, no security object. It always brought bad luck anyway.

He wanted out! He wanted to find the saboteur endangering the ship. His smart tool might have talked to the door's lock mechanism. Too bad he'd never thought to try that before. He rested the tips of his fingers near the lock, visualizing the simple latch. The door fit snugly into the wall recess. He could barely jiggle it, not enough to clear the latch. He took a turn around the room.

Loudly he said, "Screen!" and slammed his meal slot. With a quick step across the room he gave the door another jiggle. The meal slot popped open with his next ration. The screen came on. The door slid one inch.

If one inch, then . . .

He pressed fingertips to nudge it farther. There had to be emergency exits in this bucket. "No, sorry, Ship. You're no bucket. You're a beauty of design." He managed another inch. One more attempt should do it.

On second thought . . . He touched the hidden wall niche where his cleaning bot lived and pulled it out. He put the bot in his pocket. Then he got his door open.

Ran walked through the empty infirmary and into the hallway. A man stood at the intersection between two compartment modules, his hands inside an access panel.

"What are you doing?"

The man slammed the panel shut and swung around. Undergardener Blaine. Blaine who had shared Wex's toilet. Blaine who now aimed the wide muzzle of a Snub, smallest of the Subjugator line of weapons, at Ran.

A soft zzzp preceded the electrical blow that paralyzed his midsection. Paralysis prevented his crying out but didn't block the pain. Blaine grabbed him before he hit the floor. A few strides down the hallway, Blaine slid open a door, muttering, "Here I thought the others were easy compared to you, and then you walk right into my hands."

Ran landed on the floor of an empty cubicle. He listened—to the clink of a tool on the room's inner access panel, to a soft ripping sound. The room lights went off.

"Now the ship won't know you're here," Blaine said. "You spoke to Gumption and got him and Haight all riled up, ready to test everyone's excretions. I didn't know how I was going to get away, but then Renal came running to Hydroponics. I got out of there."

First Gumption, then Renal. Ran recognized the order of his calls.

"Twice now, you've made it all easy for me." The man seemed to need to talk, especially to someone who couldn't talk back.

But why the sabotage? Always why. And now what. What damage had Blaine inflicted in that access panel near the infirmary?

The door slid shut behind Blaine. A siren began howling.

Ran lay sprawled on his side, unable to move in the dark cubicle. Spasms ran through his midsection; his legs and arms twitched uncontrollably. A wonder he could breathe.

Within a few minutes, his fingertips tingled. Sensation. But his internal pain hadn't abated, and in addition—a burning in his uppermost pants pocket where he'd stuffed the little bot. It felt like the thing was clawing and eating its way into him. Blaine's Snub must have triggered some command in the bot. He had to get it out.

His shoulders prickled. Maybe he could move the arm not pinned against the floor. He raised it an inch. Another. A spasm sent it back to the floor.

Again, he inched his arm up toward his pocket, so heavy it felt like he was dragging it out of a neutron star. But up it came over his side. Inert, his hand lay on top of the pocket holding bot and knife. A spasm. The arm jerked up and down—the wrong way; it landed on the deck in front of him.

Again.

It's only pain. Get the hand in the pocket. He dragged his arm back up to his side, and bent his elbow. His next spasm drove his hand downward, where fingers caught on the pocket entrance, two inside, two out. Up. Make a fist. Into the pocket. Open the fingers. Close around the bot. Pull it out. *What relief!*

Another spasm sent the bot flying three feet to bounce off the opposite wall.

"Sorry. Sorry, sorry," he whispered.

He struggled to hands and knees, every part shaking. Then, hunched but upright, he tried the door. Even less give than his own.

If he could straighten himself, he might swing from the ceiling strap; it would make a good launching point if Blaine came back. Except there was no reason for Blaine to come back. The module had been disconnected from the ship.

How long would it take him to use up the air? Don't breathe. *Ha, ha.*

The ship wouldn't shut off the oxygen on a living body—*if* it knew he was here.

That siren made thinking difficult.

He couldn't communicate with the ship but the cleaning bot could. He forced his hand back into his pocket to pull out his knife. He opened the blade, stabbed it into his palm, and smeared his hand across the deck in one long stroke.

The siren cut off. In the sudden quiet, the hydroponics pumps vibrated underfoot.

The little cleaning bot *scritch*ed as it slowly worked on his bloodstain.

The siren resumed. What was happening out there?

Ran half crawled through the dark to feel along the wall and pried at the access panel with uncooperative fingers. Blaine had opened it easily with a tool.

Movement was getting easier. After breaking a nail, he felt for his knife with a slippery hand, wiped blood on his ship knits, and went to work. Within minutes he'd freed the cover and reached into the gap between walls, feeling for connections.

A brief arc of light. Too late. Blaine was back. No chance of reconnecting the module.

Blaine flashed a hand light on him. "Get out of there!"

In his deepest voice, Ran said, "Ship," before turning away from the wall. Hopeless. No reason the ship should hear him. He had no voice prints, no authority, nothing.

"What are you up to?" Blaine asked.

"Looking for a way to escape." Sitting on the floor, Ran rubbed his arm across his face, wiping off sweat and expression. "What are you doing to the ship?"

"Following orders."

"What orders? What have you done?"

"Since you're so good an escape artist, you can be found somewhere. Dead."

Blaine hadn't answered his question.

"How do you expect to get away with this?"

"Too late for that. I may be caught, but I'll have taken care of my mission."

"Which is?"

"To keep the cargo from arriving."

What cargo? "You mean the hibernators?" Ran got to his hands and knees. "Kill innocent people? In the depths of space? For what? You're crazy!"

"Yeah, that's what I thought when they grabbed Yvette. Said she'd be dead if I didn't go through with this. We should've turned around before we hit hyperspace. No lives lost then. But Wex got cold feet."

"You're planning to kill people." It wasn't enough that crazies did stupid things on Earth. They were spreading their craziness out into the known galaxy as well.

Blaine moved a little closer. His hand light glinted off the muzzle of his Snub. "Already done. They were the easy ones."

"You killed the hibernators?" Ran wanted to gag. Shunting horror aside, he asked, "How'd you do that?"

"Simple matter of crossing lines. Sensor says you need more O_2? The ship pumps in more—only it's CO_2, not O_2."

The siren continued to howl. Blaine cocked his head as if he were hearing it for the first time. "I guess they found 'em. You were the one in loose orbit, always in Hydroponics or talking to Gumption. I had to wait for Renal to leave the infirmary. You got Gumption all riled up, ready to test everyone. Renal went running to Hydroponics. That gave me my chance to get at you—and you walked straight to me!"

He'd said all that before. Blaine was going mad.

"How can you hope to get back to Earth if you destroy the life systems? The whole ship'll be lost!" Ran drew his legs under him in a preparatory crouch.

"Even if I don't, *she*'ll be all right."

"She who?"

"Yvette, of course. They'll kill her if I don't sabotage the ship's life systems. You think I'd do all this for nothing? They don't give you any choices, Dead Guy."

Blaine backed up. His foot landed on the cleaning bot, his hand light gyrating wildly.

Ran pushed himself up and kicked out. It might have been a perfect tae kwon do move—except for low grav and the aftereffects of being zapped.

Blaine's countermove showed he'd vexed that series far more than Ran's one-time introduction. Blaine brought the Snub around and fired at his face.

Ran screamed, but was unable to make a sound, all his senses on fire. He couldn't draw in breath.

"Where'd that bug come from? Two bugs. Three." Blaine was laughing at the approaching bots. "I'll leave you here. Machine empath eaten by machines. Perfect. I'd have had to cut you up. You solved my problem again. Let the bugs eat you."

Ran struggled but couldn't move. His breathing brought more pain.

"Don't give me any more trouble or I'll kick your head in," Blaine snarled. "I'm leaving you here. The little bugs 'll call in the big ones to help. Your puddle of digestive juices 'll feed the ship."

The siren still blared. All those dead kids.

Ran couldn't move a muscle. Like Blaine said, the little bots would find his body. They'd signal for help and the big ones would come.

"Ship!" Ran's plea was soundless. He tried again. Managed a whisper. "Ship!"

Blaine aimed his Snub again and pulled the trigger.

Aftermath

Hallie

Hallie couldn't breathe. She woke to gut-wrenching terror, far more primeval than whatever she'd been fleeing in her nightmare. She gasped and gasped for air.

A hand placed something over her mouth and nose, followed by the light pressure of a band around the back of her head. "Breathe." The person moved away.

She breathed. Her head pounded. A surge of nausea threatened. She swallowed, tried not to lose it. The ship. She was on the ship.

The siren went on and on. Above its piercing shriek, someone sobbed, loud, close by. Someone needed her help. Hallie pushed herself up to lean on her elbows, her head whirling with vertigo. She opened her eyes. A tube led from her mask outward.

Seemed like only hours ago that Pel had left her, murmuring, "Back to our coffins."

No, that was the first time. Her sleep container was open now. Nothing held her inside, except a horrible exploding head, nausea, vertigo . . .

There had been a dead bee. She hit the alarm. Pel collapsed. Was he all right?

She rubbed her eyes, glad of the dim lighting. Someone sobbed just above her. Her own spot was the bottom of three. Across from her three more units were stacked like bunkbeds. Against the pounding in her head, Hallie struggled to get her legs over the low outer ridge and took a grateful breath, clinging to the tube that fed her mask, wanting to sob in relief at breathing again.

She pushed herself out and leaned against the solid supports to touch the girl in the middle unit. With eyes shut tight against the whirling, she asked, "Are you all right?"

"No."

"I'm Hallie. Who are you?"

A sob. A mumble from beneath the girl's mask.

"What did you say?"

"I'm Reba. I feel awful."

"Me too."

A loud, firm female voice said, "Here, what are you doing?" The lieutenant popped into the little room. "Lie down."

"Just remember, Reba, we're in this together. You're not alone." Hallie couldn't help retching as she let herself be helped back into her sleep container.

"Take it slowly," said the lieutenant. "Breathe and swallow." Hallie lay back and straightened her legs, shivering.

The lieutenant raised her voice above the siren. "No one move! You hear? I'm Melissa Haight. You're all suffering from a lack of oxygen. You'll feel much better shortly, but don't fight it. Breathe. You're also cold, still coming out of hibernation. We'll be bringing you warm drinks very soon. For now, give your bodies a chance to wake up and warm up."

"Where are we?" Aryn's voice, Hallie thought, Aryn, who had held her hand while waiting for their names to be called, back at the beginning of this journey.

We're almost there. That was what the medico had said.

"We're closing in on our destination. You've been awakened slightly sooner than we had planned. Now remember, lie still and breathe."

We're in this together, she'd told Reba, but Hallie's breathing sped up. Believe it.

Long ago, she had demanded independence from her mother. Now, wherever they ended up, she'd be on her own. *Be careful what you ask for.*

Pel

Pel reached to touch his face. A hand stopped him. "Don't touch it. Breathe. It's oxygen."

His head ached abominably. He lay as still as possible so as not to disturb the throbbing. That dream again. He had to catch him, catch the guy who grabbed the card. Credits. It would take huge sums to explore the stars, to haul off dissidents, or whatever those parents of his fellow travelers represented. Huge sums had disappeared from Atlas, evaporated.

Assume AstroMining was linked to Atlas.

Assume—because he hadn't found any other contenders for the role—that the Dalguti family had inherited the wealth, the knowledge, the power. Etienne Dalguti from father Auguste from his father Pierre.

Assume Dalguti the younger still maintained control while staying undetected.

Assume Dalguti the younger had gone underground. He claimed he'd given up wealth and power. The disappearances had happened during the Dalguti father's and grandfather's time. This journey must mean they hadn't taken lives so much as stolen them.

But after the Dalguti seniors' deaths . . . Two fosterlings had come of age—and died. If those grown-up fosterlings were killed on purpose, then possibly Dalguti the younger had a different attitude toward life. Like that direflier that nearly got Ran. Pel thought he had the answers. Except the solution was on Earth. He was as far from Earth as he could possibly be.

He groaned.

"You'll be all right, Mr. Teague," said the medico's voice. "We got to all of you in time, thanks to your hitting the alarm."

No, that was Hallie's doing.

Ran

His third zap from the Snub. Ran thought he'd surely faint from the pain. But he didn't. Neither did he twitch. Every muscle in his body knotted, excruciatingly.

Blaine was running loose. A loco murderer out to kill *Orpheus* and all its passengers. Ran didn't want those unknown hibernators dead. He didn't want *Orpheus* to limp through space, poisoned, never to see Earth again.

The *scritch*ing of cleaning bots working on his blood stains comforted him. He wasn't alone. An almost imperceptible creak signaled another bot arriving through the little hatch. One bumped into his leg. Another nudged against his clenched fist. Half crawled up his hand.

That last paralyzing zap had to wear off sometime. A faint rumbling announced the arrival of an even larger bot. Were they an enlargement of the little roach shape or something else? He'd never thought to research them.

Ah well, one way or another, he'd be a part of this ship.

The door slid open. Voices. Swearing.

"Where did all these bots come from?"

"Is he alive?" came Gumption's deeper voice, just above his ship speaking voice.

Someone in a security uniform shone a light into his eye. "Yep."

"Okay. Take Wonder Boy back to his quarters."

The security officer picked Ran up—gently, he thought, though he couldn't tell, couldn't feel. Wonder Boy. He wasn't in trouble then.

Ran managed to swallow. Maybe the effects were wearing off. "The hibernators?" His question came out a garble.

Even so, Gumption seemed to understand. "No casualties, now we know you're still with us. I'll be in to question you when you've recovered."

No casualties. Take that, Blaine!

Eric Renal's examination was brief. "I've given you a muscle relaxant to counteract the Snub effects. I'll leave salve for the acid burns. Beyond that, there's nothing I can do. Rest till you feel better. Then eat. The pain will wear off eventually."

Every part of him ached. Ran moaned when he tried to get up. He'd seen grounders get Snubbed. The poor wretches now had his complete and utter sympathy. He *had* to get up. He couldn't hold it forever. Only a day ago, he'd have swung on the ceiling strap from bunk to toilet. Now he felt like a hundred fifty years old.

Gumption was leaning across his doorway when Ran hobbled back to his bunk.

"You did say no casualties?"

"Yup," Gumption replied. "So why didn't you stay safely in your room?"

Ran grimaced through his aching face. "You had a saboteur on the loose. I thought I could find him. Stupid, I know. But I did find him—Blaine—when I escaped. Did you catch him?"

"Yup." Gumption's posture imitated an old cowboy movie character, the strong, taciturn type. It didn't really fit with his small size, though. "So tell me what happened, Pawn Boy."

"I never thought it through. I got my door open, and because it was like a pet, I took the cleaning bot along. I caught sight of Blaine doing something to an access panel. He shot me and tossed me into that storage space, and then disconnected it from the rest of the ship. With no way to call for help, I gave the little bot a bit of blood to ID."

"Not bad thinking. You managed to reach all the robots on ship."

"Not true!" He couldn't have done that.

"A lot of them anyway. Quite a pretty picture, you lying there in the dark surrounded by protective robots. They not only conveyed your location to the ship but also transmitted your conversation with Blaine. More versatile than we realized."

"Oh?" He'd discovered the search and rescue function but not their ability to do voice transmissions. "Blaine wanted me dead. And all the hibernators. Why?"

Gumption looked dissatisfied. "We don't know yet. Maybe we never will until we find the ones who sent him on this mission."

"But you caught Blaine."

"We not only got Blaine, we also discovered his trick of masking his RFID chip. He thought he could sneak around the ship untraced. Didn't work this time. He's locked up beside his pal Wex."

Ran breathed out a sigh. Was the danger to the ship past? No, still the cleanup of the hydroponics system.

Gumption's cowboy pose disappeared. The second mate stood at attention. "So, Pawn Boy. First off, I owe you an apology, but you get some of the blame, calling yourself a *pawn*. I told Honey Bee that, but she insists I apologize. It was on my orders that you were confined. Blaine tipped his hand when he pulled out your smart tool. His attempt to lay the blame on you was all too suspect."

Ran jumped to his feet, ignoring screaming muscles, and looked down at the man. "You little name-caller! You might have let me know. You space turd!"

"We couldn't let Blaine suspect we were on to him, so you got locked up. And you've a long way to go to beat an insult master," Gumption said cheerfully.

Ran settled back on his bunk. He tried to scowl but his lip twitched.

"Life is unfair," the little man said.

Ran shrugged. One way or another, all his foster parents had said the same.

"But you survived it."

"Painfully," Ran answered.

"For that I'm sorry. The unexpected can't always be planned for. Oh, yeah. Here." Gumption tossed him his smart tool. Ran slipped it into the pocket of his new ship knits. "Anyway, back to my apology. Honey Bee hated to accuse you and believes the whole business cost you rather a lot of anguish. Those are her words."

Ran was glad he hadn't earned her distrust.

Gumption curled up in the doorway. "I had this idea Blaine might show us what he was really up to if we kept an eye on him, and I wanted him to think he'd gotten away with putting the blame on you. But he disappeared right when we were about to demand a specimen."

"Tell me what's been going on," Ran said.

"In answer to that," Gumption raised a thumb, "One. You escaped your lockdown."

Still holding his thumb at attention, Gumption extended his index finger. "Two. That was right after Blaine had switched the hibernators from O_2 intake to CO_2. Fortunately, a couple of them had been awakened early. They spotted the trouble and hit the alarm."

"Good work!" said Ran. What a relief no one died.

Gumption raised his middle finger. "Three. The siren sent Renal rushing back to find his sleepers dying and got to them in time."

Ring finger. "With people distracted by Blaine's antics, and no one monitoring the hibernators, it could have been a wipeout. We've all been extremely lucky."

PAWN QUEST

He waved all five fingers. "And you got Blaine to spill his secrets, which the ship recorded. He doesn't know much. We figure if the ship sends no messages, silence might keep his lady friend alive—though *he* will never enjoy her company again—unless she's some kind of soft touch."

"Or she was a plant," said Ran. Someone to seduce the man to do the will of that mastermind.

"Very likely." Gumption nodded. "In future, we need to find a way to weed out the gullibles before they get on a ship."

The second mate looked at his other hand and continued. "Blaine followed the orders of someone he calls Spider, and swallowed his capsule. After we left hyperspace, you drove him mad by keeping the sensors on the job, which prevented him from speeding up the process and forced him to plan direct murder." Still propped in the doorway, he slapped his thigh. "Everyone survived. That's the main thing."

Ran let his thoughts range ahead. "Now that I can handle VR, there's no reason I can't go to tertiary—"

"Except you're light years from Earth and we're almost to our destination. When the time comes, Ship will put in a good word for you. What do you want to study?"

"I don't know what it'd be called. Helping machines design themselves."

"One of the engineering fields, sounds like. When you get back."

"If," said Ran. He didn't know if he would be accepted in tertiary if he did get back.

As if reading his mind, Gumption said, "The ship has a fair amount of pull, especially with potential crew."

Ran straightened, with several twinges. "What about hydroponics?

That poisonous stuff is still in the system, even if you've stopped the source. Can you get it reversed?"

Gumption pursed his lips. "We hope so. Renal is taking Blaine apart—so to speak—to see what he's done to his body." He cocked his head. "Time to go. Exercise will cure your muscle aches. Let vexing prescribe something."

Ran did that, alternating meals, rest, and exercise—but the brain didn't prescribe any rock climbing, he noticed with amusement. Lots of stretches, yoga, swimming, and walks.

He lay on his bunk, contemplating his plans, feeling almost whole again. They were close to the planet. He'd caught a few glimpses of it on-screen. The crew was busy. He might have one last chance to climb that mountain all the way to its summit. Somehow, he knew he could reach the peak.

At a tap on his door, Ran looked across at Gumption.

"So, Wonder Boy Fixer, you want to finish that ship's tour we started once?"

"How can you give me a tour now?"

"Easy. We're on our way to the lander. You'll get to see every part of the ship you didn't see before. Then you can fly down with the cargo drop, a view screen all to yourself, to get a brief overview of what's known about the planet, and arrive before the others."

Ran had misjudged their proximity then. "And it's been all arranged. No choice for me?"

"You can choose this or to wait. But why wait, Pawn Boy?"

Ran stood up and grabbed his bag.

Pel

Can I see Ran?" Pel asked when they were back to breathing the ship's air again.

"He's still recovering. It'll have to wait," said Medico Renal.

"Recovering from what?" Pel asked, but the medico shook his head. "Your job is to eat, sleep normally, and vex. You and the other hibernators will have to take turns at that. We're not equipped with enough headbands for each of you."

But it seemed to Pel like they spent most of their time sleeping. He woke, ate, obediently took his turn at vexing, often someone had to shake him awake to do so, and went back to sleeping again. The hibernation habit was hard to break.

The two sexes were kept separate. He didn't see Hallie.

When he got in line to board the lander, Hallie stepped back to join him. Standing beside her filled him with a warmth that no hibernation could chill.

"So," Pel said, "How are you?"

Hallie

Hallie was glad to see Pel. The last time she'd seen him, they'd been sprawled on the floor of the girls' sleeping quarters. She considered his question.

"I never had any desire to leave Earth. When I finished secondary, I thought the world was such a safe place. Now, nothing makes sense."

"Scared?" he asked, so much sympathy in his voice that she

thought *he* might be, but what she felt was his anticipation, and something more.

Somehow his arm had crept around her waist. She liked that.

"More like angry," she answered, "because people should be able to live without being threatened and used and frightened by bullies."

"Or disappeared," said Pel.

"Or disappeared," she agreed. They were in the middle of nowhere, farther from Earth than her mind could grasp—and they had to stick together and support each other. "When I get home again, I'm going to do my part to make the world safer."

"We both will," Pel said.

She was glad he didn't point out to her that they might die here and never get back. His mystery haunted him the way her lost memory haunted her.

They boarded the lander.

Continued in Book Two

Watch for the *Pawn Quest* companion volume

Made in the USA
Middletown, DE
19 March 2022

62909061R00149